CAMP
OUT QUEST

BOOKS BY SAM HAY

Spy Penguins series:

Spy Penguins

The Spy Who Loved Ice Cream

Golden Egg

Agents of H.E.A.R.T. series:

Happily Ever After Rescue Team

Camp Out Quest

The Princess and the Pup (February 2023)

Agents of HEART

CAMP OUT QUEST

SAM HAY

illustrated by
GENEVIEVE KOTE

Feiwel and Friends

New York

A Feiwel and Friends Book
An imprint of Macmillan Publishing Group, LLC
120 Broadway, New York, NY 10271 • mackids.com

Our books may be purchased in bulk for promotional, educational,
or business use. Please contact your local bookseller or the Macmillan
Corporate and Premium Sales Department at (800) 221-7945 ext. 5442
or by email at MacmillanSpecialMarkets@macmillan.com.

Library of Congress Cataloging-in-Publication Data

Names: Hay, Sam, author. | Kote, Genevieve, illustrator.
Title: Camp out quest / Sam Hay ; illustrated by Genevieve Kote.
Description: First. | New York : Feiwel & Friends, 2022. | Series:
 Agents of H.E.A.R.T. ; book 2 | Summary: Evie goes camping with
 her family and enlists the help of friends and fairytale princesses
 in a quest to get her stepmother to fall in love with the stray puppy
 she wants to keep.
Identifiers: LCCN 2021049707 | ISBN 9781250798312 (hardcover)
Subjects: CYAC: Magic—Fiction. | Princesses—Fiction. | Fairy tales—
 Fiction. | Camping—Fiction. | Cooperativeness—Fiction.
Classification: LCC PZ7.H31387385 Cam 2022 | DDC [Fic]—dc23
LC record available at https://lccn.loc.gov/2021049707

First edition, 2022
Book design by Liz Dresner
Feiwel and Friends logo designed by Filomena Tuosto
Printed in the United States of America by LSC Communications,
Harrisonburg, Virginia

ISBN 978-1-250-79831-2 (hardcover)
1 3 5 7 9 10 8 6 4 2

ISBN 978-1-250-79832-9 (paperback)
1 3 5 7 9 10 8 6 4 2

For Alice and Archie, always my inspiration

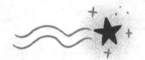

CHAPTER 1

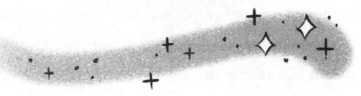

Evie took a deep breath, then reached for the plate of cherry pie. *This is it. Can Wonder Waitress do the triple table drop-off without spilling anything and take the gold in the Super-Server Olympics?* She slid the plate of pie carefully under her thumb and little finger on her left hand. Then she added a plate of peanut butter brownie bites, which she balanced on the wrist of the same hand. Lastly, she picked up a bowl of Happily Ever Ice Cream, her brand-new recipe invention, and held it tightly in her right hand. She glanced up at her stepmom, Hannah. "Does this look okay?"

"Perfect!" Hannah smiled. "Now keep your head up, walk straight, and take it nice and slow."

Evie grinned and resisted the urge to give her stepmom a thumbs-up. *Okay, table eight, here I come!*

With a few waitressing tips from her stepmom and A LOT of practice that morning, she was starting to get the hang of it . . . *I've only had two minor slippages today,* Evie thought as she set off across the room, carefully balancing the plates. *And neither of them was more than a 3 on the OMG Accident Scale! But don't be overconfident,* she reminded herself. *Because that's when it all goes—* "Whoa!" she breathed as she nearly tripped over a purse one of the diners had left by their table. *Focus, Wonder Waitress!* She glanced back over her shoulder and gave Hannah a reassuring smile, then set off again—

—And nearly walked smack bang into a customer who was standing up to take off his jacket.

Wowzers, that was close, Evie thought, ducking under his long, outstretched arms. *Not far now . . . only three more tables to get past . . .*

But just when she was starting to pick up speed, a lady suddenly leaned back in her chair . . .

"Whaaa!" Evie gasped as she did an emergency stop, narrowly avoiding a crash. Her plates wobbled wildly but didn't fall. *Breathe, Wonder Waitress! Come on, you're so close now . . .*

Evie continued on her way, carefully stepping over lumps of squishy fries that a toddler was lobbing off his plate and avoiding a leaking ketchup packet that had fallen off a table. But her arms were getting achy now, and her hands were beginning to shake with the weight of the plates. She gritted her teeth. *Nearly there, just a few more steps . . . can Wonder Waitress make it over the line . . .*

—YES SHE CAN! And she takes the gold! "Hi there!" she said as she reached table eight. "Here's your order. I hope you enjoy it." She laid the plates down with a bit of a bump, but no spillages, then glanced

across the room to Hannah and gave her a triumphant smile.

Her stepmom beamed back and mouthed, "Well
done!"

HOW TO BE A SUPER SERVER BY EVIE BROWN

Waiting tables takes loads of practice
and a whole lot of skills. But my stepmom,
Hannah, gave me a few tips that really help.
She says the best way to remember them is
by spelling out her most important rule of
all . . . SMILE!

 is for smile! Because no one wants their meal ruined by a grumpy server. And if you make your customer feel happy by being happy yourself, they'll definitely want to come back again.

 is for menu. Know your menu inside and out so you can recommend specials and tell your customer what is in all the items on the list.

 is for individual. Each customer is different. Whether it's a bored preschooler or a family celebrating or a person in a rush. Adapt your service style to meet their demands.

 is for listen. Some customers can't eat certain things. Others have strong preferences. Be sure to listen when they tell you what they need.

 is for explain. If things go wrong (and when I'm in the diner, they usually do), sometimes all you need to do is explain the problem, apologize, and make it right. Most customers are very understanding.

Evie felt her chest puff up with pride. *Could this day get any better?* She turned to check the nearby tables to see if there were any dirty dishes to clear, just as her stepmom always did, and considered how awesome this Saturday was shaping up to be. First, Hannah had agreed to let her help out in the family diner all day. Then her dad had suggested they put Evie's new ice cream recipe as the top item on their daily specials board. And as if that wasn't enough, there was Fudge . . . Evie smiled dreamily at the thought of the shaggy, stray pup. He'd unexpectedly appeared the day before, thanks to the Agents of H.E.A.R.T.: a team of rescue princesses that had popped out of a magical book and turned her life upside down.

Evie glanced at the clock on the diner wall. *Just ten more minutes, then I'll take my break and go wake Fudge.* She felt a warm glow inside as she pictured the pup upstairs, curled up peacefully in his box in the Browns' apartment above the diner. Except Fudge wasn't curled up peacefully in his box.

Evie heard a sudden scrabbling of paws as a blur of brown fur streaked across the floor, along with the loudest *Hi-Evie-I-was-getting-a-little-bored-and-lonely-upstairs-so-I've-come-to-find-you* sort of a bark, as Fudge dived through the diner and threw himself into her arms.

"Oh my goodness," Evie gasped as the pup licked her face from top to bottom and then back again, wagging his tail and woofing with joy. "Um—hi, Fudge! How did you get in here?"

All around the room, people were looking and staring and grumbling . . .

Evie gulped. *Quick, Wonder Waitress, Apologize and Explain.* That was what Hannah said to do when things went wrong. "I'm so sorry . . . ," she told the customers. "This is Fudge. And he's absolutely, definitely NOT allowed in here!" She glanced across the room at her stepmom and felt her tummy flip-flop. *Uh-oh, that is not a Happy Hannah face!*

When rescue princess Agent B had brought her Fudge, the fluffiest of fluffy puppies, it was love at first sight for Evie. But her stepmom had been reluctant to let him stay, because "Dogs aren't allowed in the diner."

But Evie was doing her best to change her stepmom's mind. *And this really isn't helping*, Evie thought. *But maybe the Apologize and Explain strategy could still work?* Evie smiled at the customers. "See, I promised Fudge a walk in ten minutes, only I don't think he's learned to tell the time yet. But I'm going to take him right out of here, so please carry on like you never saw him, like he was never here. Thank you very much."

She hugged the squirming pup closer, gave her stepmom a reassuring nod, and set off across the diner, her head held high, as though she was a waitress who was in charge of everything that happened, and nothing—not even the wriggliest, jiggliest puppy on the planet—was going to put her off.

But as Evie passed one of the tables, Fudge got a sniff of something tasty on a diner's plate, and with a sudden lunge, he shot out of her arms like a slippery bar of soap and landed heavily on the shocked customer's lap.

"Fudge! NO!" Evie cried.

But it was too late. The pup had already helped himself to the lady's hot dog, and in one quick gulp, it was gone.

For a second, the whole room seemed to stop. Every head, every face had turned to stare at the mega disaster that was unfolding at table three.

Okay, so this is actually a 10 on the OMG Accident Scale. And I'm really not sure "Apologize and Explain" is going to be quite enough this time. There was only one solution: EVACUATE!

Evie grabbed Fudge off the lady's lap. "I am so sorry!" she said, not even starting on the "explain" part of the strategy, and raced for the front door of the diner, which by some miracle actually opened in front of her.

"Hey, Evie!" Her friend Iris stood in the doorway with Iris's cousin Zak just behind. "We've got the most exciting news ever!"

CHAPTER 2

"*The most exciting news ever*" *is definitely an improvement on the last thirty seconds*, Evie thought as she staggered out onto the café's patio with the fidgety pup in her arms.

"Er—did something bad just happen?" Zak asked, peering through the windows into the diner. "Because that customer is looking like she swallowed a hornet."

Evie didn't want to look back, but she forced

herself. She saw her stepmom by the customer's table, looking like she was trying to smooth things over. From the way the woman was on her feet with her hands on her hips, it didn't seem to be going well.

"So I'm guessing Fudge decided to help himself to that lady's lunch?" Iris suggested. "Because he's looking kind of guilty." She stroked the pup's head and he gave a sorry little whine.

Evie sighed. "No matter how hard he tries to be good, when it comes to hot dogs, he just can't help himself."

"It's not Fudge's fault," Zak said, tickling the pup's ears. "Dogs are basically just wolves, and wolves have an instinct to survive. And I'm sure when you've been living behind a trash can for months, like Fudge has, you take every opportunity for food whenever it appears."

Not that Hannah will see it like that, Evie thought. Fudge was only supposed to be staying with the Browns for the weekend until he could be dropped off at the pet shelter on Monday. Evie had been hoping that if he behaved well, he'd be able to stay forever. But that plan seemed to be sinking faster than a chocolate soufflé with a fork poked into it.

"I know something that will cheer you up," Iris said.

"You do?"

"Sure . . . it's the exciting news I was telling you about. There's this awesome forest scavenger hunt today, up at Big Woods . . . and we want you to be on our team."

"Me?" Evie smiled. She loved scavenger hunts. There had been one every year at her old school before they'd moved to Lime Bay. And last time Evie had come in third, winning a glow-in-the-dark T-shirt and cap.

"Sure, and Alex says there's a really good prize for the team that comes in first," Iris said as though she were reading Evie's mind.

"Alex is our big cousin," Zak explained. "He's a Junior Ranger up at Big Woods, and he designed the scavenger hunt. He knows everything about animals," he added proudly.

"But how will we get up there?" Evie's face clouded over. "Because my parents are really busy today and I don't think I'd be allowed to cycle that far and—"

"Gammy's going to take us!" Iris interrupted. "She's going to get someone to watch her stall so she can drive us."

Evie glanced across the street to where Gammy, Iris and Zak's grandma, ran her flower business. "Oh, that's so kind of her. And it really does sound fun!"

"What sounds fun?" said a voice from behind Evie.

She spun around. "Dad!"

Ben Brown had appeared from the diner, still wearing his chef's apron. He smiled at Iris and Zak, then looked at Evie. "So I heard there has been a bit of an incident with Mr. Dog . . ." He reached over and tickled Fudge, whose tail began to wag. "I know I'm a good cook, little pup, but you've got to learn not to eat everything I make!"

Evie giggled. "It was a bit of a disaster."

"Well, dogs like to be outdoors and running around," her dad said. "Not stuck in a boring apartment by themselves, right, boy?"

Fudge's tail began to wag faster, and he let out an excited little bark.

"Hey—maybe you could bring him on the scavenger hunt," Iris suggested.

"What scavenger hunt?" Hannah had appeared behind Evie's dad.

Evie noticed her stepmom's hair was disheveled and her face was red. "Smoothing over" the Fudge catastrophe had obviously been tricky.

Iris coughed. "Me and Zak are going on a scavenger hunt up at Big Woods today, and we wondered if Evie—and Fudge—could come, too."

Hannah's shoulders seemed to relax a little. "Oh, well that sounds like a nice idea. You could definitely do with using up some of that puppy energy!" she added, giving Fudge a half smile. "Are dogs allowed in the woods?" she asked Iris.

"Sure! And Gammy won't mind Fudge coming along."

Hannah nodded. "Okay, well, I'll go have a word with your grandma to make arrangements . . ."

"Wait up—" Evie's dad had a thoughtful look on his face. "How about we ALL go up to Big Woods today?"

"What?" Hannah frowned. "But we've got the diner to run, and Saturdays are always so busy and—"

"And we deserve a rest." Evie's dad put his arm around Hannah's shoulders and gave her a hug. "How about we close early today, dig out the tents, and have a night under the stars up at Big Woods. Everyone says it's a magical place."

"A camp out?" Hannah's eyes lit up. "Well, I guess we haven't had a day off for months . . ."

"Can Iris and Zak camp, too?" Evie blurted out. "They can sleep in my tent."

"Oh, well, I don't know . . . ," Hannah began.

"I LOVE camping!" Iris said.

"Me too!" Zak said. "And Gammy can give permission for me to go. I'm staying with her for the weekend while my parents are away—"

"—and if we go with you guys, Gammy won't have to find someone to mind her stall!" Iris added.

Evie felt a surge of excitement now. "And if Iris and Zak come, there'll be more people to look after Fudge, because he can come, too, can't he?"

Hannah's face softened. "Well, I suppose he might be a whisker less trouble in the outdoors."

"Oh, he will," Evie said. "You'll be as good as gold, won't you, boy?" *For starters, there'll be no customers he can steal food from. And if this camping trip works out, maybe Hannah will see what a lovely pet you are, and we'll be your fur-ever family. Fingers and toes and paws and tails crossed!*

CHAPTER 3

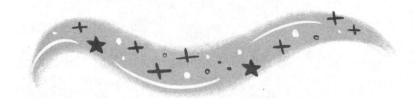

"So I'm going to bring all sorts of food with me, because I love camp cooking . . . Did I tell you that? . . . And I'm planning loads of dishes . . . like popcorn . . . pancakes . . . muffins— Do you guys like s'mores? Because I do, and I have so many recipes and—"

"I'll bring my new camera!" Zak interrupted Evie. "And my binoculars, because there's all sorts of wildlife up at Big Woods, and—"

"Headlamps!" his cousin Iris butted in. "We'll need to take some of them with us, because midnight tag is just the BEST game in a dark forest. And if you put on high-vis vests, you can totally find people and—"

"AND you guys are really loud!" Gammy laughed. She bent down to pat Fudge, who was sitting under her flower stall. "You are definitely going to need doggy earmuffs if you're going camping with these three!" She smiled up at Hannah. "It's so kind of you to take Iris and Zak with you. Are you sure you don't need to borrow anything . . . extra camping gear, maybe? Or I could contribute to the food?"

"Oh, it's fine, thanks," Hannah said. "We used to do a lot of camping before we moved to Lime Bay. We just need to shake the dust off the tents . . . and we've got plenty of food in the café. By the sound of it, Evie's already planning the menus." She smiled at her stepdaughter. "I'm quite glad. Her campfire popcorn is absolutely delicious. Now I'd better get back to the diner . . ."

"And I'd better help this lady with her purchase," Gammy said, smiling at a customer who had appeared behind Hannah. She glanced at Evie, Iris, and Zak. "How about you guys go make your plans on the beach."

Fudge let out a bark of happiness as they walked down the steps from the boardwalk. The pup seemed to enjoy the feeling of the sand under his paws.

Me too, Evie thought as she slipped off her sandals and picked them up to carry. *The beach is definitely one of the best things about moving to Lime Bay!*

When Evie's parents had first suggested they relocate to the seaside town of Lime Bay and buy a diner, Evie had thought it was the most exciting idea ever. It combined a lot of her favorite things: sea, sand, and sundaes! Especially the sundaes. Inventing new desserts was what Evie was best at. But she'd soon learned that running a café was hard work. Plus, her parents hadn't initially wanted her to help out in the diner, so she'd felt lonely upstairs in the apartment by herself. *But not anymore*, she thought, glancing at her new friends. *Thanks to the Agents of H.E.A.R.T., now I'm allowed to work in the diner and I've got you guys to hang out with—and Fudge!*

"Hey, I've just thought of something awesome!" Iris said, stopping to knock over a large lumpy mound of sand. "We won't have to be on litter-picking duty."

Zak's eyes sparkled. "Oh yeah, I'd forgotten about that. Wow! This weekend just keeps on getting better."

"Um—what's litter-picking duty?" Evie asked.

Iris grimaced. "Gammy runs this beach cleanup club to remove any trash left lying on the sand."

"And we were supposed to help this weekend," Zak added. "But now we're going camping . . . we'll be too busy!"

Evie grinned. "So have you camped out at Big Woods before?" she asked them.

"Oh, loads of times," Iris said. "Last time my parents came home we stayed up there for a week.

Mom and Dad brought their guitars and they did this mini concert for all the campers."

Evie smiled. She was looking forward to meeting Iris's parents next time they returned to Lime Bay. They were traveling musicians and away a lot, so Iris lived with her grandma.

"Big Woods is great for wildlife spotting," Zak said. "Alex told me he'd found some moose droppings a few days ago. Maybe we'll find some, too."

"Ew!" Iris made a yuck face. "What is it with you and poop? Zak is always looking for it," she added, turning to Evie. "Last weekend he was collecting owl pellets around Gammy's farm. So ick!"

"No they're not!" Zak glared at her. "You can learn all sorts of scientific things from owl pellets; once I found a whole mouse skeleton inside one."

That does sound kind of cool, Evie thought.

But Iris's face was all scrunched up. "Gross!"

"There's nothing gross about anatomy," Zak snapped. "And mice are awesome. Alex told me they have more bones than we do! And hey—maybe Alex will have put owl pellets on the scavenger hunt list today!"

 # HOW TO DISSECT AN OWL PELLET BY ZAK FLOWERS

If you're as fascinated by animal anatomy as I am (unlike Iris!), you'll really enjoy dissecting owl pellets. Remember, pellets are the regurgitated remains of an owl's meal; they're not poop! Owls spit out the pellets after eating. (Imagine what Gammy would say if I did that?)

Lots of birds produce pellets, and you can discover a whole lot of interesting things about what species made the pellet by seeing what it ate. You may find entire skeletons of small mammals! But first you need to have good hygiene. Make sure you wear gloves and wash your hands well afterward.

- You can find pellets in forests, or your local owl conservation group may be able to give you some.

- Store your pellets in an airtight container until you're ready to dissect.

- Soak your pellet in a dish of water and a little disinfectant before dissecting.

- Soaking the pellet for 24 hours will loosen all the little bones inside.

- Useful tools: a small twig or stick to probe your pellet. Tweezers. Magnifying glass. Small mammal and reptile identifying guide.

- Consider mounting your bones on cards to display.

For more information, check out Canada's Science World and the UK charity Barn Owl Trust.

"WHAT? NO WAY!" said a sharp voice from behind them. "Don't tell me YOU'RE doing the scavenger hunt at Big Woods today, too!"

Evie spun round and saw not just one cranky face, but two. *The Pemberton twins!*

As well as making two new friends in Lime Bay, Evie had also made two new enemies: Katie-Belle and Clara Pemberton. Their parents owned a luxurious rival café a few yards up the street from the Browns' diner, and they weren't the biggest fans of Evie and Fudge. Especially not after Evie and her family had beaten them in the Golden Coffee Cup Best Café Contest!

"Yeah, we're doing the scavenger hunt," Iris said. "AND we're camping out, too!" she added proudly.

Clara looked at her sister. "I'm so glad WE don't need to stay in smelly tents anymore, aren't you?"

"Ugh, yes!" Katie-Belle pretended to shiver at the thought. "Our parents have just bought a top-of-the-line RV. And we're taking it up to Big Woods tonight. And it's got a rainfall shower, a real kitchen, and four proper beds!"

Zak chuckled. "Sounds like you're just taking your house."

"Well, it's better than being bitten by bugs all night!" Clara smirked at her sister. "AND it's got a big table, so we can lay out everything we find for the scavenger hunt. Because we're going to ace the competition."

"I bet we can beat you," Iris blurted out. "Right, guys?" she glanced at Zak and Evie.

"I guess," Zak murmured.

"Um—sure," Evie said.

"Challenge accepted!" Clara said. "If we win, we get to think up a forfeit for you."

"And WHEN you lose," Iris told the twins, "we'll think of one for you!"

"Um—is this such a good plan?" Zak whispered to Iris. "They could dream up something really nasty."

But Iris and Clara were already shaking on it.

"Ooh, I know what their forfeit can be," Katie-Belle said, her eyes glinting. "Dishwashing!"

"Huh?" Iris glanced at Evie and Zak.

"Awesome idea!" Clara said. "See, our café's dishwasher is broken and it's not getting fixed until next week, so you guys can come by and wash all the dishes."

"No way!" Zak said.

"Too late," Clara said. "We shook on it. See ya later, losers! Oh, and don't forget your rubber gloves, Zak."

"Um—guys," Evie whispered as the Pembertons stalked off across the sand. "I don't mean to worry you, but there are A LOT of dishes to wash in a diner."

"Don't worry," Iris said. "There's no way we'll lose. I know those woods like the back of my hand."

I hope you do, Evie thought. *No way do I want to be helping out a rival diner by washing their dishes! I want to be working in our diner. And besides, if I'm stuck at the Pemberton place, who'll look after Fudge?*

CHAPTER 4

"Smoky and sweet popcorn topping . . . ," Evie said, reading off the long list she'd written.

"Um—yep, I think so?" Iris held up a tub of brown granules, squinting at them suspiciously. "But they don't look yummy."

"Maybe not. But they taste amazing!"

It was a little while later, and the friends were back in the Browns' diner, packing up food supplies in the kitchen.

"Popcorn kernels?" Evie said. "Extra-large bag?"

"Here!" Zak put them into the cardboard box on the counter.

"Marshmallows?" Evie said.

"Half a bag." Zak held it up. "Or more like a third of a bag."

"Mmm, not enough . . . ," Evie said. "Can you get some more from the pantry? It's just down the hall. Oh, and graham crackers, too . . ." She glanced back at her list. "Chocolate sauce?"

"None that I can see," Iris said, looking along the counter.

"That's in the pantry, too," Evie said. "And I also need a bag of caramel chunks and lots of bananas. We'll use them in the banoffee pancakes."

"Are you guys nearly done?" Hannah poked her head around the kitchen door. "Oh my word!" she gasped, seeing the amount of food in Evie's box. "Are you planning on feeding the entire campground?" She chuckled. "Two more minutes and then we've got to go. We want to get up there before it's dark."

Evie quickly added a pot of honey and a large bag of flour, then some extra blueberries. She was just wondering whether she should put some bagels in, when Iris returned with a large bunch of bananas, as well as the other ingredients Evie had asked for. She squished them all into the box.

"I got the marshmallows," Zak said, following his cousin back into the kitchen. "But one packet looked a little small . . ."

"So you brought three?" Evie laughed.

"Well, Zak can usually manage a whole pack of marshmallows by himself," Iris said. "Before breakfast!"

"Very funny! Do you need anything else?" Zak asked Evie.

She hesitated. There *was* something else, something extremely important. Though she wasn't sure how popular it would be with her friends. *But I can't go without it!* She reached into a kitchen drawer where she'd hidden it under the tea towels that morning. As she pulled it out, Evie heard Iris groan.

"Nooo! Not the magical fairy-tale book!"

For once Zak agreed with her. "That thing's nothing but trouble."

Evie remembered how they'd both told her about being visited by the agents before Evie had met them and neither had enjoyed the experience much. "I know the agents can be a little chaotic . . . ," she began.

"That's an understatement," Zak muttered.

"But we might need them!" Evie said. "And they can be so useful. Remember how they helped me persuade my parents to let me help out in the diner?"

"They also turned Fudge into a donkey," Iris said.

"And gave you crazy long hair!" Zak added.

Evie reached up and touched her head. It was true, her neck still ached a little after spending the day before with a giant braid stuck to her skull. "But it's back to normal now."

"Um—hello?" Iris said. "It's still orange!"

Evie grinned. "I kind of like that."

"Face it," Iris said. "Trying to keep the agents in check is like herding cats."

"But they're also so much fun." Evie looked at the picture of the rescue princesses on the front of the book and smiled—*Huh? Did Agent C just wink at me?* That was the thing about the book. You never knew what might happen next. "Guys, we've got to take it with us. It's a real live magic book! What if someone snuck in here while we were gone and took it?"

"If only!" Iris muttered. "Have you forgotten how the agents never listen to you?"

"And they always argue!" Zak added.

"And their ideas are so"—Iris frowned—"old-fashioned!"

"Don't worry. I've got something that will make sure they pay attention to me." Evie opened another kitchen drawer and began rooting around inside.

"Hey—are you guys done yet?" Evie's dad appeared in the doorway, his arms full of sleeping bags. "Because Hannah and Fudge are already in the car."

"Coming . . . ," Evie said. But she'd still not found the thing she needed.

"I'll carry the food." Zak went to pick up the food box—

"Or maybe not!" Iris laughed as he tried—and failed—to lift it. "Let me help," she said, reaching for one end and ignoring her cousin's scowl. "Come on, Evie," she added as she and Zak lugged the box toward the door. "We've got a scavenger hunt to win."

"Sure, just one moment—" *Gotcha!* She smiled as she found the thing she'd been looking for and shoved it into her backpack along with the fairy-tale book. Then she took one final look around the kitchen, just in case there was anything else that might come in handy for her camp cooking. "Okay, I'm ready!" she told the empty room. *Ready to make amazing food! AND win a scavenger hunt! AND, most important, convince Hannah to let Fudge stay!*

CHAPTER 5

"Wow!" Evie breathed, craning her neck up and turning around slowly in a circle. "Some of these trees look taller than skyscrapers!"

"Well, maybe not THAT high." Ranger Alex smiled. "But yeah, several of the fir trees here are nearly three hundred feet tall, maybe more."

It hadn't taken them long to drive up to Big Woods. But, although it was only a few miles above Lime Bay, the two places couldn't be more different.

"Most of the trees are old, right, Alex?" Zak said, pulling his camera out of his pocket to take pictures.

"Yep, there's one near your campsite that is thought to be more than five hundred years old."

"Whoa." Evie giggled, looking at her parents. "That's even older than you guys!"

They all laughed, and Evie noticed how relaxed her parents looked. Ever since they'd left Lime Bay and taken the road up through the forest to the campground, they'd both been goofing around and joking a lot more than usual. Her dad had dug out his old, battered panama hat that he always wore when they went camping. And Hannah had tied her hair up in a pretty pink scarf with cherries on it. Evie had even seen her stepmom bending down to tickle Fudge's ears once or twice. *Now that we're away from the diner, Hannah really seems to like Fudge a lot more*, Evie thought as the pup trotted by her stepmom's side. *Maybe persuading Hannah to let him stay isn't going to be as hard as I thought.*

"So there's another block of showers down at the other end of the campground," Ranger Alex was telling them. "And if you want any trail maps, just come by my office. Oh, and here are your scavenger hunt sheets," he added, handing them to Iris, Zak, and Evie. "You can draw or take photos of the things on the list. Deadline for entries is six p.m. The Head Ranger will judge the contest. And there's a big box of camping goodies for the winner!"

THE BIG WOODS SCAVENGER HUNT

BIG WOODS

Scavenger Hunt List
— Photos or drawings —

Bird	Campfire	Beetle	Grasshopper
Butterfly	Orange-Colored Leaf	Unusual Shaped Stone	3 Feathers
Seedpod	Fungi	Putting Trash in a Trashcan	Mammal
Pawprint	Bark Rubbing	Creative Camp Food	Tree Selfie
Cobweb	Burrow	Caterpillar	Bird's Nest

HOW MANY CAN YOU FIND?

"Can we work as a team?" Iris asked, handing back two of the sheets.

"Sure. And you can check off the first item on the list as soon as you get your campfire going."

Iris looked at Zak and Iris. "Quick! Let's go find firewood . . . It's got to be dry, with no mold or moss on it; I learned that at Scouts. Pine burns well but makes a lot of smoke—Zak? Are you listening?"

He was on his hands and knees peering at the ground. "Nope, because I just spotted the most amazing beetle . . ."

"That's a jewel beetle," Alex said, looking over his cousin's shoulder. "You could add that to your scavenger list, too."

"Awesome, I'll take a photo of it."

Iris pulled a pen out of her bag and checked it off. "One more item closer to beating the Pembertons!"

For the next half hour or so, they all got to work setting up camp. Evie loved this part of camping: pitching the tents, lighting the fire, laying out all the supplies. *And most important, planning the food,* she thought as she unpacked her cooking supply box.

"Can you put this pan on the fire for me?" she asked her dad as she poured in a bag of popcorn kernels and a splash of oil. "I can't wait for everyone to have some." *Especially you!* she thought, looking at her stepmom, who was relaxing in a foldout chair now, taking photos of their campsite on her cell, with Fudge lying by her feet. *Whoa! She's definitely in her happy place now,* Evie thought. Hannah's "happy place" wasn't an actual location. It was the feeling her stepmom had whenever she was relaxed and peaceful. And Evie knew that the best time to get Hannah to agree to anything was when she was in her happy place. *So that's where she's going to stay!* Evie thought, popping a lid on the pan and handing it to her dad. *And being served a whole bunch of yummy snacks while sitting in her favorite comfy camping chair will definitely help keep her there. Then I can ask her about keeping Fudge . . . Come on, Super Chef, you've got this!*

Her dad gave the popcorn pan a shake to separate the kernels, then reached for the thick fire glove. "I'll swap the pan for the pot," he said, taking the metal coffeepot off the grill and pouring out two cups for him and Hannah. "You kids help yourself to a soda. They're in the cooler."

Zak looked up from the bug book he was reading and nodded. But Iris wasn't listening. She had borrowed Zak's binoculars and was peering off into the distance. "I just saw the Pembertons," she whispered to Evie and Zak. "And they look like they've already ticked off a whole heap of stuff from their scavenger list. Come on; I really don't want to be washing dishes in their diner!"

Nor do I, Evie thought. *Because if I'm stuck at the Pembertons' place all day, Fudge could get up to all sorts of trouble. And NO WAY would Hannah want to keep him then.*

"Just a few more minutes," she told Iris, "and the corn should start to pop. Maybe we should give it another shake?" she asked her dad.

But as he reached for the pan, there was a loud *CRACK!* as the kernels began to explode against the lid. Fudge let out a yelp of fright. He dived away from the fire toward the trees, trailing his leash behind him.

CHAPTER 6

Evie leaped forward, knocking over Hannah's coffee cup, which had been sitting on the grass by her stepmom's chair. "Fudge!" she yelled. "Stop!"

But the pup had now vanished into the trees.

"FUDGE!" Evie yelled louder. "COME BACK!"

"It's okay," Evie's dad said. "He won't be far away."

"But Fudge doesn't know the woods," Evie said. "He might get lost."

"Don't worry. I'll go get him."

As he ran off down the trail after the pup, Hannah put her arm around Evie's shoulders. "I'm sure Fudge won't have gone far . . . try not to fret . . . but really, Evie"—she paused and sighed—"this is part of the reason why we can't keep Fudge. He's just too young and excitable. Imagine if he ran off when we were working in the diner . . . we wouldn't have time to go search for him. And he could easily have an accident on the roads in Lime Bay."

"But I wouldn't let that happen! I'd always keep Fudge safe." Evie couldn't believe what she was hearing. *We've only just arrived and Hannah's already made up her mind about Fudge!* She gritted her teeth. *It's not over yet! There's still time to show her how amazing he is and how well I can look after him.* "Maybe we should go help Dad," she called to Iris and Zak.

"Okay, but don't go far!" Hannah said. "I don't want to lose you guys, too!"

"Fudge! FUDGE!" Evie yelled as they raced down the forest trail. But even though she listened really carefully, there was no friendly *woof* in reply.

"I guess he could be anywhere," Iris said as they came to a split in the path.

"Well, he definitely went this way," Zak said, bending down to check a muddy patch. "Look, you can see his paw prints."

"How do you know they're his?" Iris asked. "They could belong to a squirrel, an otter, a raccoon . . ."

Zak snorted. "If that paw print belongs to a squirrel, we're in big trouble; it would have to be a monster-size squirrel to leave a print so large. And otters tend to be closer to water. And as for a raccoon . . . their prints look more like hands. Wait—I've got a book in my backpack on tracking animals. I'll show you . . ."

HOW TO MAKE
A PAW PRINT PLASTER CAST
BY ZAK FLOWERS

A great way to help you identify animal tracks is to make plaster casts of the prints you find. Then you can take them home and research the shape and size of the track to learn what creature made it.

You will need:

- Plaster of Paris
- Water
- Cardboard
  - Gloves

- An old container to mix your plaster in
- A stick or spoon or old paintbrush to stir the plaster
- Newspaper to wrap the print in

Method:

- Find an interesting animal track. (Slightly soft, mushy ground is best.)

- Clear any rocks or grass out of the track, being careful not to damage it.

- Surround the print with a cardboard collar. (This is a long rectangular piece of cardboard you can use to put around the print to isolate it.)

- Put on waterproof gloves.

- Mix up the plaster of Paris with water (according to the instructions on the packet) in your container.

- Fill the collar to cover the print, with extra on top.

- Let the plaster set. It takes about 20-30 minutes to become soft set. If you can leave overnight, even better.

- Poke the cast gently with a stick to see if it's set.

- When it is, carefully move your cast. Take care, because it may still be soft.

- Wrap it in paper and take it home.

- If you want, you can paint your finished cast.

Evie glanced over his shoulder as he opened his backpack. "Whoa, it looks like you've got a whole library in there."

Zak blushed. His parents owned a second-hand

bookstore, and Iris always said he read every book that came in. "Well, you never know what information you're going to need." He pulled out a wildlife guide and began leafing through it.

But Evie was distracted by something else. Her nose had started to twitch. "Hey, do you guys smell that?"

Iris sniffed the air. "Hot dogs?"

"Yeah, I think so," Evie said. "And remember what happened on the beach yesterday?"

Zak looked up. "What happened on the beach yesterday?"

Iris rolled her eyes. "I've told you that you should get out of the bookstore more!"

"Guys!" Evie said, trying to stop an argument before it started. "See, Fudge took off like a rocket when he smelled the hot dogs at the beach snack bar yesterday," she explained to Zak. "And then this morning, remember how he wolfed down that customer's hot dog in the diner . . . So I was thinking maybe the same thing has happened now."

Zak nodded. "Dogs do have a powerful sense of smell."

"And very greedy tummies!" Iris added.

"Come on, let's go see." Evie led the way off the path, following her nose. They crossed through some thick bushes and low branches until they reached a break in the trees where they could see smoke coming from someone's campsite. But as they stepped into the clearing—

"Oh my word!" Evie gasped, her eyes wide, her mouth opening in horror. "Fudge!"

He was up on his back legs pinching food off a table covered in a bright yellow cloth.

Evie blinked at the scene. She noted the fancy RV parked close by. And the four foldup chairs set around the table, two of which were bright pink with the initials *KB* on one and *C* on the other. *Oh no! It can't be . . .*

Just then, a familiar blond-haired lady appeared from the door of the RV carrying a large tray of buns. She froze when she spotted Fudge.

"Mrs. Pemberton?" Evie gasped.

Zak groaned. "Of all the hot dogs Fudge could have found!"

CHAPTER 7

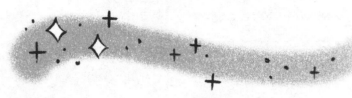

At the sound of their voices, Mrs. Pemberton spun around. "Is this your dog?"

"He's mine!" Evie squeaked. "And I'm SO SORRY." She rushed forward and took hold of the pup's trailing leash. But as she tugged him away, his mouth was already full of hot dog.

"Don't worry," Evie said. "We can cut off the bits he's chewed . . . I did that this morning with Dad's breakfast pastries and he didn't notice at all."

Mrs. Pemberton glared at her. "Where is your mom? I've got a few things to say to her!"

The walk back to their camp felt like the longest few minutes of Evie's life. No one spoke. And Fudge crept alongside Evie with his head drooping and his tail between his legs. *Quick, Super Chef! Think of some way to rescue the situation . . . Wait!—I know . . .* She took a deep breath. "So—um, Mrs. Pemberton—I've been making my secret recipe camp-corn popcorn," Evie began. "And I was thinking maybe you'd like to try some? Maybe you could even take some back for the family? I'm sure the twins would love it and—"

"No thank you. We don't eat popcorn."

The way she said that made popcorn sound like boiled slugs! Evie took another deep breath. "Well, I could make you some s'mores instead. I've got these awesome flavor combinations."

Mrs. Pemberton made a *harrumph* sort of a noise. "No thank you!"

Evie noticed the woman's mouth had grown smaller and tighter, and her frown had become deeper and darker. And by the time they reached the Browns' campsite a moment later, Mrs. Pemberton appeared to be shaking like a volcano about to explode . . . And then she spotted Hannah and did!

"How dare you let your dog run wild!" Mrs. Pemberton blurted out. "He stole the meal I was preparing for my family, right off our table."

Hannah's eyes goggled. "Oh my goodness, I am so sorry . . . but he wasn't running free. You can see, he's still got his leash on . . . He was tied up, but he got scared and then he pulled it free and ran off and—"

"No excuses!" Mrs. Pemberton snapped. "He might have bitten someone."

"He wouldn't do that," Evie said. "Fudge only likes cuddles and food."

"I find that hard to believe. He was like a wolf with my hot dogs!"

"Strictly speaking, wolves are shy and gentle," Zak said. "They almost never attack humans and—"

"What's happening, Mom?" The twins had

sneaked up behind their mother, and they now appeared at her side, their eyes sparkling with glee at the sound of all the drama.

"That monster stole our hot dogs!" Mrs. Pemberton cried, pointing a finger at Fudge, who slunk behind Evie to hide.

Clara put her hands up to her face and gasped in mock horror. "What? Oh, but that must have been *soooo* scary for you."

"Especially since Dad hasn't arrived yet," her sister Katie-Belle added. "He's still working," she told Hannah. "Because our café is soooo busy and soooo popular!"

"Yeah, and what with me and Katie-Belle off walking around the campground, finding ALL the items for the scavenger hunt," Clara went on. "We're actually nearly done now," she said, smirking at Iris.

Katie-Belle wrapped her arms around her mom and hugged her. "You're so brave, Mom. Imagine having to fight that beast off all by yourself!"

"Quite right," Mrs. Pemberton said. "Which is why I'm going to inform the Ranger," she said, scowling at Hannah, "and have you all thrown out of the campground. Come on, girls, let's go!" And she turned and stomped off with the twins behind her.

Hannah gave Fudge a hard look. But the pup, who was peeking around the side of Evie's legs now, didn't meet her gaze. "I guess I should go to the Ranger's office, too. Evie, tell your dad where I am if he gets back before me. Oh, and you kids better start packing up. We'd better go see if we can drop Fudge off at the pet shelter today. For his own safety," she added, giving Evie a sad but firm look.

"Aw, we won't win the scavenger hunt now!" Iris wailed as soon as Hannah was gone.

"And I definitely won't see a moose," Zak groaned.

"And we'll have to help Gammy with the beach litter-picking!" Iris added.

"And I'm going to lose Fudge!" Evie gasped. "And

that's WAY worse than any of those other things." She crouched down next to the pup and hugged him tight. "I know it wasn't your fault about the hot dogs, boy. If people are silly enough to leave food lying around, what can they expect?" He gave her a lick and wagged his tail. But even he seemed a little glum, as though he knew what was about to happen to him.

This is not fair! Evie felt a surge of energy in her belly. She clenched her fists and lifted her chin. *I'm NOT going to let Mrs. Pemberton take you away from me!* She reached for her backpack and pulled out the magical fairy-tale book. It felt warm in her hands, and the cover seemed to shine brighter in the sunlight.

"Oh no!" Zak said. "Not that."

"Stop!" Iris said. "The agents will not make this better."

But it was too late—Evie was already saying the words . . .

CHAPTER 8

"I WISH I COULD STAY IN THE CAMP SO HANNAH CAN'T TAKE FUDGE TO THE PET SHELTER!"

There was a loud cracking sound, a flash of silver light, and the sweet smell of magic filled the air. Then—

"You're here!" Evie gasped as three Agents of H.E.A.R.T. appeared in front of her.

"Well, of course we're here," Agent R said, flexing her muscles and doing a few leg stretches. "That's how enchanted books work, right?"

"Um—sure," Evie said. "Only, I wasn't sure it would work for a second time."

"Oh, Evie," Agent C said, shaking out the skirt of her long pink frock and smoothing it down. "It'll *always* work. Forever and ever!"

Iris and Zak groaned.

Not that Agent C seemed to notice. "And now we should introduce ourselves."

"Is that necessary?" Agent R said. "Evie knows who we are."

"But we've been practicing a new introduction!" Agent C did a little spin on the spot so her frock billowed out, then she struck a superhero pose. "Well, hello there, Little Miss Smart," she said, smiling at Evie. "You've asked for help from the Agents of H.E.A.R.T.!"

Agent R scoffed. "So silly!"

"I like wands and magic, and my name is Cinderella . . . ," Agent C went on. "And if you're making pizza, I love mozzarella!"

"Great rhyme!" Iris giggled.

"Your turn." Agent C pointed to Agent R, who tossed her long silvery locks over her shoulder, then flexed her biceps.

"Rapunzel's my name, I'm very good with hair, I find it very useful if there isn't any stair!"

Evie looked at her friends and grinned. "I love this!"

"Ooh, ooh, my turn now," said the third agent. "My name is Beauty and I love a warm jacuzzi, sewing is my hobby and I'm often rather snoozy!"

Zak cocked his head to one side. "Er—who is she?"

"Dunno," Iris whispered. "But she's definitely NOT Beauty."

"Ah, but I *am* Beauty." The unknown agent winked at them.

Evie peered at her more closely. *She doesn't LOOK like the Beauty we met before . . .*

This agent wore a sparkly onesie sleepsuit with little moons on it. On her feet were glittery slippers. And on her back, she carried a giant purple backpack with a sleeping bag tied to the bottom.

"Oh, wait!—Are you SLEEPING Beauty?" Evie asked.

"Sure am." The new agent grinned. "Agent S at your service."

"Oh wow, I love the Sleeping Beauty story," Evie breathed.

"Really?" Agent R frowned. "But all she does is prick her finger and fall asleep. It's snore-some!"

Agent S poked her tongue out. "Not as snore-some as long hair and tall towers."

"Yes, yes. So about your wish, Evie . . ." Agent C stepped past the other two. "You want to stay at the campground, right?"

Evie nodded. "But my stepmom wants to leave and—"

"Don't worry, kiddo," Agent R said, shoving Agent C out of the way. "We'll lock her in a tower!" She pointed to Zak. "You! Lend me those glasses." Without waiting for Zak to agree, Agent R whipped the binoculars from around his neck and peered through them, scanning the campground. "There's bound to be an empty tower around here somewhere."

"Oh, we don't need a tower," Agent C said, gliding past Agent R so she was in front once more. "We'll just put your stepmom in a giant pumpkin coach until she changes her behavior."

"Or a tent?" Agent S pitched in. "You seem to have two very good ones here," she added, patting the roof of the closest one. "And I'm an ace at sewing, did I tell you that? We'll pop both your parents inside and stitch up the flap until you want to go home."

Agent R snorted. "Tents? Pumpkins? Don't be ridiculous! They'd escape in seconds. We need bricks and mortar, and maybe some bars at the window."

"Er—thanks, but I don't really want to put my parents in prison," Evie began.

But the agents were too busy bickering with one another now to hear.

Zak shook his head. "See? This is what always happens!"

"Yep. Just like last time," Iris added. "They never listen."

But Evie DID listen. She'd paid a lot of attention to her friends' opinions of the agents when they'd appeared before. And this time she was prepared. *No way are the agents going to ignore me today*, she thought, *not when I REALLY need them.* She reached into her backpack and found the thing she'd brought from home. *Okay, here goes!*

CHAPTER 9

PEEEEEEEEEEEEEEEEEEEEEEEEEEEEEEEEEEEEEEEEEEEE
EEEEEEEEEEEEEEEP!

Evie blew on the whistle she'd brought as loudly as she could.

Fudge dived under a chair. Zak and Iris clamped their hands over their ears. And the three rescue princesses froze.

"Sorry about that," Evie said, climbing up onto a log. "But please could you all listen? My parents will be back at any moment—and no thank you, I DON'T want you to lock them up," she added as Agent R tried to interrupt. "You see, I need to stay at the campsite so Hannah can't take Fudge to the pet shelter. I want her to spend more time here so she can get to know him better." She smiled at the pup, who was poking his head out from under the chair now. "And hopefully that will make her change her mind about letting him stay. So please could you all help? Maybe you could even work as a team this time?" she suggested hopefully.

The agents looked at one another with confused expressions.

Okay, so maybe team *isn't a word in the rescue princesses' dictionary!* Evie thought.

Agent S put her hand up to ask a question. "May I taste some of your corn?" She pointed to the table where Hannah had placed Evie's popcorn in a bowl. "It smells divine."

"Um—okay."

"Here we go again," Agent R muttered. "You always get distracted by snacks."

"That's because I'm writing a slumber party recipe book with my friend the V.U.P.—that's the Very Useful Prince," she added, her eyes twinkling at Evie. "He's so much more helpful than his cousin the Handsome Prince! This popcorn looks so delicious—mmm," she murmured as she swallowed a few pieces. "I LOVE it!" As she said the word *love*, a tiny red embroidered heart shape appeared above her head and then popped.

"That's so cool!" Evie breathed.

Agent S's eyes sparkled. "Ooh, but not as cool as your popcorn. It's smoky AND sweet! You must tell me how you made it."

 # EVIE BROWN'S SUPER-SPECIAL CAMP-CORN RECIPE

Popcorn is one of my all-time favorite camping snacks. I love the sound of it crackling in the pan! If you want to make some, you'll need a grown-up to help with the hot bits, plus a lidded pan or a roll of aluminum foil. Here's how I do it.

Ingredients:

- Popcorn kernels

- Vegetable oil

- A campfire or stove

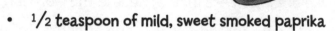

- $1/2$ teaspoon of mild, sweet smoked paprika

- 1 tablespoon of brown sugar

- 2 tablespoons of maple syrup

- A grown-up!

How to make:

- Put 1 tablespoon of vegetable oil in the pan.

- Add popcorn kernels (enough to cover the bottom of the pan in one layer).

- Cover the pan with the lid.

- Ask your grown-up to put the pan on the grill or the campfire. (If you don't have a pan, you can make individual foil parcels—one for every person in your group.)

- The corn should begin to pop after a few minutes.

- Get your grown-up to gently shake the pan to make sure all the kernels pop.

- When pan has stopped popping, remove from the heat and tip popcorn into a large bowl.

- Mix the paprika and brown sugar together. Add the syrup, then stir over your warm popcorn and serve.

· * ✳ ☾ ✳ * ·*

"Later!" Agent R scowled at her. "First we've got to focus on helping Evie with her problem."

"Agreed!" Agent C said.

"And I know exactly what we need," Agent R

went on. "A tower! A big, tall, intimidating tower."

The other agents groaned.

"Not to lock Evie's parents inside." Agent R folded her arms huffily. "But to give Evie and Fudge somewhere to hide. And then when your parents come to take the pup, we'll pour stuff out the window on them . . . like pigeon poop!" Her eyes glinted. "Or itching powder. Or molasses! That'll make them change their minds."

"No, no, no!" Agent C said. "That's ridiculous! We just need to make a pumpkin coach and we'll

lock Evie's stepmom AND Fudge inside and send them off somewhere until they become the best of friends."

Evie cocked her head to one side. *Would that work?*

"You're both wrong!" Agent S murmured, staring at the bowl of popcorn with a thoughtful look on her face. "We need an idea that will make Hannah *want* to stay at the campsite, and I know exactly how to do that . . . We'll throw a slumber party! A spectacular super-special woodland slumber party, right here in the forest."

"Huh?" Agent R grunted. "And you said my plan was silly."

But a slow smile was spreading across Evie's face. "I think it's a brilliant idea."

Everyone stared at her. Everyone apart from Agent S, who let out a loud *whoop* and began doing a crazy jogging-on-the-spot sort of dance move.

"You see, Hannah really likes camping," Evie explained to the others. "And she really likes parties. So if we combine the two things, she'll never want to leave here ever again."

Zak frowned. "Have you forgotten we're about to leave to take Fudge to the pet shelter, like RIGHT NOW?"

Evie's smile slipped a little. "Yeah, I guess that is a problem . . ."

"Not necessarily," Iris said. "We just need to come up with a few delaying tactics; like when it's bedtime, but you really don't want to go, so you suddenly find loads of urgent tasks to do, like checking your backpack, or clearing out your pencil case or discovering that your cat's coat *really* needs brushing— What?" she said, looking at Zak, who was frowning at her. "You do that all the time! Like last Sunday when you *really* didn't want to help Gammy wash up, so you suddenly found an exciting beetle in the yard that you just had to identify."

"It was a shiny scarab beetle," Zak said. "And Gammy thought it was cool, too."

Iris rolled her eyes. "Whatever! But you guys

will help delay Evie's parents, right?" She looked at the agents hopefully.

"Of course *they* will!" Agent S answered on behalf of the other two agents. "While I plan the party. After all, it's my skillset."

Agent R snorted. "Personally, I don't like parties. All that standing around with cake and conversation. I prefer action: white-water rafting, rappelling, bareback horse riding—"

"I love parties!" Agent C interrupted. "Though I never get to stay to the end."

Agent S looked at the others. "That's because of her midnight curfew," she mouthed to them. "Well, don't worry," she said in a louder voice. "You won't have to leave early today, because this is Evie's story, not yours! Now, the most important thing is to make sure we invite EVERYONE! Especially any bad fairies that you might know," she added, her face suddenly a little anxious. "Because sometimes they get into such a big huff when they're accidentally left off the guest list." She laughed nervously.

"Stop! No invitations!" Agent R bent down and picked up a pine cone. "You can't have a party because it's going to rain . . . See how it's all closed up? That's a sure sign."

"It's not going to rain," Agent S said. "The sky is all sunny and lovely and perfect for an outdoor slumber party."

Agent R folded her arms. "Excuse me, but which one of us has their own meteorological station on the top of their tower AND presents their own weather channel?"

Evie, Iris, and Zak looked at one another. *Rapunzel was a weather forecaster?*

"That wasn't in any book I ever read," Iris muttered.

Agent S sighed. "Rapunzel, you're such a gloomy-shoes! It won't rain. Now, come on, let's start planning our party . . . but first we'll need to get the campsite cleaned up. Agent C, you'll be great at that, what with all that dusting and polishing you do for your stepmom. And Agent R, you'll be brilliant at making the campsite look less drab—after all, you spend so much time in boring towers, you must know how to dress them up!"

"And I'll do the food," Evie said. "I've brought loads of ingredients—"

"We'll help you." Iris suddenly looked excited. "And if we can win the scavenger hunt, too, we'll have a whole box of camping goodies to use for the party."

"Ooh—I like scavenger hunts!" Agent R said, rolling up the sleeves of her frock and cracking her knuckles. "Gimme the list and I'll have the whole lot found for you in ten minutes flat."

Iris's eyes goggled. "Oh wow, yes, please! It's here—"

"No thank you!" Agent S snatched the list out of Rapunzel's hand. She folded it in half and handed it back to Iris. "First we've got to help Evie." She gave Agent R a stern look. "Because EVIE made the wish."

"Quite right!" Agent C said.

Agent R sniffed. "Some of us can multitask, thank you very much."

"Now—back to party planning . . . ," Agent S said, ignoring her. "I know exactly what we need . . . Some decorations. Garlands! Cushions! A lovely, snazzy tablecloth!" She heaved the backpack off her back and unzipped it. "Luckily, I never travel anywhere without my sewing machine. Did I tell you I LOVE sewing?" As she said the word *love* again, another little red embroidered heart shape appeared in the air above her head before it popped. "I'll make a tablecloth and napkins, too—oh, and I'll sew everyone a sparkly onesie, just like mine—even you, little doggums," Agent S said, patting Fudge on the head.

The pup let out a whine and Zak grimaced. "I'm fine without a onesie, thanks very much."

"Nonsense! Now, can I use your tent?" Agent S asked, already unzipping the flap. "I've got heaps of fabric in my backpack, so I can get started right away."

"Um—hello!" Iris said. "There's still the small problem about how we're going to stop Evie's parents leaving."

"Yep, and that problem is on its way over here right now," Zak added. "Look!"

Everyone turned to see Evie's parents walking back toward the campsite; Hannah's face was grim, and Evie's dad's shoulders were slouchy.

"No!" Evie gasped. "I won't let them take Fudge away. Anyone got any ideas?"

"Hide their car keys?" Iris suggested.

"Run off into the woods?" Zak offered.

"Lock them in a pumpkin coach?" Agent C tried again.

Agent R grunted. "None of the above; leave this to me."

Uh-oh, Evie thought, *why don't I like the sound of that?*

CHAPTER 10

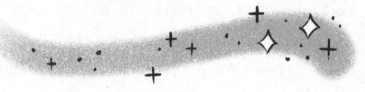

Agent R stalked across to where Evie's parents had parked their vehicle and crouched down by one of the tires and began to fiddle with it.

"Is she doing what I think she's doing?" Iris whispered.

"Yep," Zak said. "It's actually quite a clever plan."

Evie gulped. "But my parents will be mad when they see—"

"See what?" said a voice behind her.

Evie spun around to find her dad looking down at her. "Um—"

Iris coughed. "One of your tires is flat."

"It is?" Evie's dad glanced across to the parking lot. "Mm, it does look a little soft."

As he walked over to check, Agent R had already moved onto the next tire. Not that Evie's dad could see her—the agents were invisible to grown-ups.

"Okay, everyone, let's get packing," Hannah said. "If you kids start taking your tent down, I'll do this one." She reached down and pulled out a peg and her tent sagged a little.

Evie looked at Iris and Zak for help. If they collapsed their tent, what would happen to Agent S, who was inside right at that moment, sewing party garlands?

Iris winked at her, then—"Excuse me, Mrs. Brown," she said. "But when we were at the pet shelter yesterday, it looked awfully busy. They probably wouldn't have room for Fudge today."

"Thanks, Iris, but I called when I was over at the Ranger's office, and they said they'd squeeze Fudge in."

What? Noooo! Evie couldn't believe what she was hearing. *Hannah had already arranged to drop Fudge off? This was a total disaster.* "Oh, Hannah, please can we stay here just a little longer?" *At least long enough to let us plan the slumber party that will make you want to stay in the campsite forever!*

"I'm sorry, honey, but no." Hannah wrestled the next tent peg out of the ground, and the tent drooped even more. "If Fudge runs off again he might get hurt." She stopped fiddling with the tent for a moment and crouched down to stroke Fudge's head. "I know he's cute. But we just don't know enough about dogs to care for him properly. If he escapes again, Mrs. Pemberton will probably hand him over to the police!"

Evie shuddered at the thought. "But you won't run off again, will you, boy?" She crouched down and put her arms around him. The pup let out a sad little whine, as though he'd try his best, but he couldn't be sure, though he wished he could. Evie looked up at Hannah. "I promise to keep Fudge on the leash at all times and—"

"Unbelievable!" Evie's dad called over. "They're all flat!"

"What?" Hannah turned to look.

"The tire pump is missing from the trunk, too." Evie's dad shook his head. "I just don't understand it."

Evie tried not to smile. Agent R was standing right beside her dad now, and Evie was pretty sure she was hiding something behind her back.

"I'd better call the garage," Hannah said, reaching into her back pocket. "Oh, that's odd . . . where's my cell?"

She cast around, looking for it. But Evie realized it wasn't the only thing that had vanished.

Where's Agent C? Evie wondered. *I hope she hasn't gone off to find a pumpkin to lock my parents inside.*

"I'm sure I left it on the table," Hannah said,

crouching down on her hands and knees to look underneath it.

"Mine is missing, too," Evie's dad said as he walked over. "I had it in my pocket a moment ago . . . but now it's gone."

"Fudge will find your cells!" Evie blurted out. "He's a sniffy dog. And dogs are renowned for their powers of smell, right, Zak?"

"Huh? Oh—um, yeah." Zak nodded. "I read this magazine once that said a dog's sense of smell is a hundred thousand times more powerful than ours."

"That's great," Hannah said, rummaging inside her backpack now. "But I don't really think they can find cell phones."

"Fudge can!" Evie said. *And then you'll see how useful he can be.* She felt a tingle of hope in her tummy now. *Maybe if you think he's a helpful pet, you'll want to keep him.*

"Perhaps I left it in the Ranger's office?" Hannah said, running her hand through her hair.

"Or maybe you dropped it on the way back from the Ranger's office," Evie said. "And someone else picked it up, thinking it was their cell . . . Come on," she called to Iris and Zak. "We'll go take a look around camp." She grabbed Fudge's leash and her backpack, and began walking away before her stepmom could stop her. "So what we're looking for is a cell about this size"—she held out her hands to show her friends exactly how big—"in a bright yellow case . . ." She deliberately made her voice extra loud so she couldn't hear her stepmom if she was calling after her. "Once Fudge picks up the scent, we're bound to spot it easily."

"And on the way, we can pick up some more items for the scavenger hunt," Iris added.

"AND we might even see a moose!" Zak said, slipping the lens covers off his binoculars.

And the longer we take, Evie thought, *the longer we've got to plan the best party EVER, which will stop Hannah from taking Fudge to the pet shelter.*

CHAPTER 11

"Can dogs really find cell phones?" Iris asked Zak.

They were out of Hannah's sight now, walking down one of the tree-lined paths surrounding the campground.

Zak nodded. "I read that some police dogs can detect the chemicals on the coatings of electronics devices."

Evie looked at Fudge, who had his nose stuck in

an old candy wrapper he'd found on the ground. "Can all dogs do that?"

"I guess they need to be trained first," Zak said.

Iris giggled. "Fudge is definitely trained for snack recovery. Maybe he could work for the FBI—the FOOD Bureau of Investigation."

Fudge looked up at the sound of his name and wagged his tail, with the wrapper still stuck to his nose.

"More like the CIA," Zak said. "That's the Candy Intelligence Agency!"

Evie chuckled. Fudge did look ridiculous. She bent down to remove the sticky wrapper. "There, that's better, isn't it, boy," she said as she went to put the wrapper in a nearby trash can.

"Stop!" Iris said. "I think we need a piece of trash for the scavenger hunt." She peered at her list. "Yep, here it is: 'putting trash in a trash can' . . . Thanks, Fudge!" She gave the pup a tickle. "Maybe you're a better tracker dog than we thought—Zak, take a picture of Evie putting it in the trash can."

"It's just like being part of Gammy's litter-picking group!" Zak grumbled.

"Don't remind me about that," Iris said. "Come on, let's go find more things on the list."

For the next ten minutes, the friends zoomed around the campground looking for Hannah's cell and finding items on the scavenger hunt list, including a grasshopper, a brightly colored butterfly, an orange leaf with green veins, an unusual stone shaped like Fudge's head, three different feathers, including one that Zak said belonged to a hawk, a giant seedpod, and an odd-looking fungus . . .

"Don't touch it!" Zak said as Evie and Iris bent down to get a closer look. "That's a death cap mushroom. Highly poisonous!"

"We're not idiots." Iris rolled her eyes. "Here, give me your camera and I'll take a picture."

"So I was wondering, Evie," Zak asked. "If we lose the scavenger hunt, just how bad would washing dishes at the Pembertons' diner be?"

"Well, take your worst chore ever and multiply it by a million."

Zak's eyes goggled. "Really?"

"Sure! For starters there's the giant kitchen pots and pans. They're WAY bigger than the ones you have at home. And so much dirtier. And just lifting them is a bit of a struggle . . ."

"Ugh!" Iris grimaced. "I hate washing dishes. All those icky little bits of food floating around in the water."

"And your hands get so red and wrinkly, even if you wear extra-thick gloves."

"Like prunes!" Iris said. "I hate prunes."

Evie nodded. "When we first moved into the diner, we didn't have a dishwasher. It was such hard work for my parents—"

"Look!" Zak interrupted, craning his neck and staring up into the tree they were standing under. "I think I just spotted an owl. There!"

"Oh wow!" Iris said, peering at it through the camera lens. "That ticks off another item from the list."

"And check out this bark," Evie said, running her hand over the tree. "It looks like dinosaur scales. We should do a rubbing for the spotting sheet." She dropped her backpack on the floor and rummaged inside for a pencil.

"You know, this tree would be ideal for the selfie, too," Iris said, looking up into the branches.

"Huh?" Zak frowned. "What selfie?"

"It's on the list," Iris said, holding up the sheet to show him. "'Tree selfie.' And this one looks easy to climb."

"But who takes the photo?" Evie asked.

"The self-timer." Zak reached for his camera and fiddled with the buttons on the back. "Okay, you guys start climbing while I set it up."

"What about Fudge?" Evie asked.

"Tie his leash to a branch near the bottom of the tree," Iris suggested. "Then he can be in the shot, too."

"Okay, be a good boy now," Evie said, wrapping

the pup's leash tightly around a low-hanging tree branch before she clambered up onto another branch to join Iris.

"Come on, Zak!" she called to her cousin.

"Okay, okay. I've never used the self-timer before." He propped the camera up on a log a little distance away, then raced over to join them. "I think it gives us twenty seconds," he puffed as he scrambled up next to them.

"How do we know when to smile?" Evie asked.

"Watch that light on the front," Zak said. "When it stops flashing, that's when it takes the picture."

But just as the light changed, there was a sudden noise from the bushes by the camera, and two figures shot out in front of the lens, blocking the shot.

"Oops!" Clara Pemberton said. "Did we interrupt something?"

Zak frowned. "We're trying to take a picture."

"Oh, was it your tree selfie?" Clara said, looking from them to the camera. "We took ours ages ago."

She glanced at her sister, who smirked back. "Sorry we spoiled your shot."

Iris's eyes narrowed. "What were you doing crawling around in the bushes anyway?"

"Just looking for the last things we need for the list," Katie-Belle said, her face reddening.

"More like spying on us, to see what we've found!" Iris whispered to Zak and Evie.

"Oh, is that the naughty dog?" Katie-Belle said, wandering over to where Fudge sat patiently at the bottom of their tree.

He looked at her, and his tail began to wag . . . but she ignored him.

"Cute leash," Katie-Belle said, running her hand along it to where it was tied to the branch.

"I'd better go reset the camera," Zak said, starting to climb down.

"No, no, it's okay," Clara said, picking it up. "I'll do it for you."

"What? No!" Zak said.

CLARA PEMBERTON'S SUPER SELFIES!

Me and Katie-Belle are aces at taking selfies; we're so much better than Iris Flowers and her new friend, Evie. Their selfies are soooo dull! If you want to be a super selfie taker like me and Katie-Belle, try out some of these awesome poses. But don't forget to get the lighting right. If you're indoors, turn toward the light. If you're outside, make sure you're not squinting into the sun, otherwise you'll look really silly, just like Iris and Evie.

- Take a mirror selfie. Bonus points if it's a cute mirror.

- Stick out your tongue. Or touch your nose with your tongue if you can stretch that far!

- Instead of a picture of your face, take a picture of just your shadow.

- Blow bubbles in your selfies.

- Take a spoon selfie, showing your reflection in the metal.

- Puddle reflections are fun for selfies, too.

- Find a funny background. If you have a plant behind you, you can make it look like it's growing out of your head.

- Try a hand or foot selfie. Accessorize with rings and bracelets or colorful socks or sneakers.

- Do a barefoot selfie and paint each toenail a different color. Or paint smiley faces on your toenails.

- Take a selfie of your feet in different locations.

- Get your BFFs together and take a group shot.

- A group selfie of just your feet is awesome, too.

- Angles are cool! Try tilting your camera to the side. Or hold it above your head and look up.

- Take a "shelfie" of your favorite books.

- Try taking lots of pictures in the same location with different hairstyles, accessories, or expressions.

- Pose with pets. (But not hot-dog-munching naughty dogs like Fudge! YUCK!)

*** ✳ ☾ ✳ ***

But Clara was already fiddling with the buttons on the back. "Oh dear," she murmured. "That's not good."

"What's wrong with it?" Zak jumped down from the tree and raced over.

"Well, I think I might have accidentally deleted some of your scavenger hunt pictures."

"What? Let me see!" Zak reached for his camera while Iris and Evie climbed down after him.

Clara chuckled. "I really hope I haven't lost any of your extra-special pictures."

"They're ALL gone!" Zak gasped. "The beetle. The owl. The grasshopper. The butterfly. The trash can shot, the—"

"No way!" Iris glared at Clara. "How could you?"

"It was just an accident." Clara looked at her sister. "Tell them, Katie-Belle; I'm not the best with technology."

Her twin's eyes sparkled. "Oh, that's *soooo* true! Clara's absolutely hopeless with cameras. I've taken all our scavenger hunt pictures, haven't I, Clara?"

"Then why did you offer to help?" Iris said through gritted teeth.

Clara shrugged. "Just trying to be friendly. But if you don't want our help . . ." She tossed her hair. "Do it yourself next time! Come on, Katie-Belle, let's go finish our hunt."

Iris glared at them as they stalked off. "Ugh!"

she groaned. "They're so horrible. I'm sure she did it on purpose!"

"Are all the photos gone?" Evie asked Zak.

"Yep, she's completely erased every picture we took."

"I can't believe it!" Iris wailed. "Now we're going to have to wash dishes in their stinky diner. That's even worse than helping Gammy clean up the beach."

"Don't worry," Evie said, trying not to let her voice sound as wobbly as she felt. "We've still got the drawings we made on the spotter's sheet. And the things we put in my backpack, like the pebble, the feathers, the leaf—"

"But we need all the photographs, too!" Iris said. "And we may not be able to find all the things again . . . Like that awesome giant cobweb and the hairy caterpillar with the stripy body."

"We can take more photos now." Evie pointed to one of the trees. "Look—there's a cobweb. It's not as big as the one we had before, but it's still really sparkly."

"And we can get that poisonous mushroom again," Zak said, walking over to take a picture. "And we can retake the tree selfie."

Iris nodded. "Okay, let's do that one now."

Zak placed his camera back on the log and set it to self-timer, again, while Evie and Iris clambered up into the branches.

"Good boy, Fudge," Evie called down to the pup. "We won't be long."

"Ready?" Zak said as he scrambled up next to them. "Okay, everyone, smile."

But the moment the camera shutter clicked, Fudge's ears pricked up. He twisted around to look at something through the trees. Then suddenly he let out a loud bark, tugged his leash free, and took off like an arrow from a bow.

For a heartbeat, the friends just sat in the tree looking at one another, then—

"Quick!" Evie yelled, jumping out of the tree. "We've got to get him back."

CHAPTER 12

Evie's heart felt like it was doing a super-fast drum solo at a rock concert. *What if we can't find him? What if he steals more hot dogs? I'll never get Hannah to fall in love with him then.*

Head down, arms pumping, she chased after the pup, jumping over tree stumps, swerving past bushes, and nearly falling over an anthill! *I just don't understand how he got free,* she thought as she dived over a fallen log. *I tied his leash so tightly and—*

"There he is!" Zak yelled. He veered off to the left, pushing his way through some tall ferns. "Fudge!" he yelled. "Stop!"

The pup did exactly what he was told and skidded to a halt underneath a large tree.

Zak made a dive for the pup's leash, throwing himself onto the ground. "Gotcha!"

"Perfect timing!" called a voice from above, and Agent R poked her head out of the leaves. "I knew if I whistled for Fudge, you'd all come running. Now, catch this, will you . . ." And she lowered a large branch toward Zak.

"Whoa," he gasped, as the weight of it nearly knocked him over. "Hey, you guys," he called to Evie and Iris, who had arrived by his side now. "Help me!"

"What on earth—" Iris reached up and took the middle of the branch while Evie caught the other end, and together they wrestled it down to the ground, just as Agent R somersaulted out of the tree.

"Um—what are you doing?" Evie asked.

"Building!" Agent R said, grabbing the heavy branch with one hand and hoisting it up onto her shoulder. "And this old broken branch is ideal!"

"Are you making something for the slumber party?" Iris asked.

"Ha!" Agent R tossed her silvery hair over her shoulder. "I told you, that's not going to happen. There's rain coming."

"Then what *are* you building?" Zak said.

Agent R tapped her nose and grinned. "A surprise! But it's going to be big AND tall!"

Evie froze. *Uh-oh! That sounds exactly like a tower.* "Er—that's great, only I really don't want you to lock my parents up, thanks. You see, we're planning a spectacular slumber party instead, so maybe you could build something nice for that and—"

"Sorry, got to go!" Agent R walked off, dragging the giant branch behind her.

"This is not good," Evie said.

"Well, it's not all bad," Iris said. "Look what Fudge just found." She crouched down next to the pup, who had his nose stuck in a hole in the ground. "Some sort of burrow, maybe?"

"Fox, probably," Zak said. "I'll take a picture." But as he checked his pocket for his camera . . . "Huh? I must have left it back where we took the selfie."

"And my backpack, too," Evie said. "Come on, let's go get them."

They retraced their steps back through the ferns and along the path, with Fudge obediently trotting beside them and Evie keeping a tight hold of his leash. But when they got there . . .

"It's gone!" Zak cried, looking around the log. "I definitely left my camera here."

Evie glanced around, a flush of worry on her face. "My backpack's missing, too . . . unless we've got the wrong place," she added hopefully. "All these trees look the same."

"Nope, this is definitely the right place," Zak said. "See, there's the tree we took the selfie on."

Evie felt a wave of panic now. "But I can't have lost my backpack. It's got the magic book inside!"

"And all our things for the scavenger hunt," Iris wailed. "The feather, the leaf, the pebble . . . Wait!—Where's the spotter's sheet? Have you still got that?"

Evie shook her head. "I left that next to my backpack. It's gone, too."

Iris's eyes goggled. "But we NEED that sheet!"

Evie bit her lip. "Will your parents be mad about the camera?" she asked Zak.

"Nah! Because it won't be lost. Someone probably just picked it up, along with the sheet and your backpack, and turned it all in to the Ranger's office. That's what I'd do if I found someone's stuff. We should go check."

Zak's right. I'm sure we'll get it all back . . . But what if they didn't? Evie's mouth suddenly felt dry. "I can't believe I've lost the magic book," she murmured.

Iris shrugged. "Well, I guess every cloud has a silver lining. Now maybe someone else will have to put up with the annoying Agents of H.E.A.R.T.! Fingers crossed!"

CHAPTER 13

As they made their way across the campground to the Ranger's office, Evie couldn't stop thinking about the book. She knew her friends found the agents annoying . . . *But my life is so much more exciting with the agents in it,* she thought. *Spending time with real magical beings is the best thing that's ever happened to me—well, apart from Fudge.* She glanced down at the pup and his tail began to wag. Evie walked a little faster, trying not to imagine what would happen if the person who had found the backpack made a wish on it today. *Would the agents suddenly vanish from the campground? And what about the slumber party? Without the agents, I won't be able to keep Hannah here, and then I'll lose Fudge forever. I've got to get that book back!*

"Oh hello, slumber-party team!" Agent S stepped out of the bushes in front of them.

Oh phew! Evie thought. *The agents are still here! For now, anyway.*

"I'm just off to find some more fabric," Agent S said. "I've made so many things for the party . . . sparkly garlands, bright cushions, pretty napkins, and the most beautiful cozy throws for the chairs, perfect for slumber party stargazing."

"Hannah loves looking at stars," Evie said. "We got her a telescope for her last birthday." With all the worry of losing the book, she'd put the slumber party at the back of her mind. But talking about it made her feel more positive.

Agent S was on tiptoe now, glancing around

the campground like a onesie-wearing meerkat. "I need more fabric for the sleepsuits," she explained. "I've used up every scrap of material I brought with me. But you can't go to a slumber party without a super-special outfit."

Zak grimaced. "But there aren't any fabric stores here. It's just tents and trees."

"Stores?" Agent S giggled. "Oh, I never get my fabric at stores. I just reuse things I find. I LOVE recycling."

As she said the word *love*, the little red embroidered heart appeared above Agent S's head again.

Evie smiled. *I love it when that happens.*

"But what can you find in the forest to make into clothes?" Iris asked. "It's just a bunch of leaves and trees, and moss and flowers . . ."

"Oh, you'd be surprised at what you can find if you look hard enough," Agent S said. She winked at them. "Sometimes the best things are right under your nose. Now, I must fly!" And she dashed off into the trees.

HOW TO MAKE A SWEET-SCENTED HANGING HEART
BY AGENT S

If you aren't able to make magical hearts appear above your head like I am, don't fret. Here's how to make a sweet-smelling fabric heart to give to your friends and family.

You will need:

- Pretty fabric or felt (I like to recycle old pieces of material.), enough for two 6-inch (15-centimeter) squares

- 5 inches (12 centimeters) of ribbon

- Needle & cotton thread

- Pins

- Toy stuffing (or old pantyhose could work just as well)

- Dried lavender or rosebuds

- Chalk or pencil

Method:

- Cut two 6-inch (15 centimeters) squares of fabric and put them together, right sides facing in.

- Draw a heart shape to fill the fabric.

- Then draw another heart shape inside the first one, to create a seam allowance— about 0.2 inch (5 millimeters).

- Cut out the hearts on the outer line.

- Pin the pieces together.

- Sew the pieces together using a backstitch, but leave a little gap (approx. 1 inch or 3 centimeters) to stuff the heart.

- Turn the heart inside out, so the right sides of the fabric are showing.

- Stuff the heart, adding a few pieces of dried lavender or rosebuds. Sew up the gap.

- Loop the hanging ribbon and sew the ends to the top of the heart.

NOTE: If you want a neater finish, you can leave a small gap at the top of the heart when you sew the pieces together. Then after you have turned it right side out and have stuffed it, you can tuck the ends of the ribbon into this small gap and sew up to attach the ribbon.

✳ ∘·∘◇ ✳·∘◇✳ ∘·∘◇ ✳

"I'm looking forward to seeing our leafy one-sies," Iris said. "What about you, Zak?"

But her cousin was staring across to the Ranger's office. "Whoa," he muttered. "It looks like the whole campground is in there."

Not just inside. Outside, too! A long line of cranky-looking campers was forming outside the Ranger's office door, and as the friends got closer, they could hear people grumbling about having lost things . . . Cell phones, clocks, watches . . .

Just at that moment, Ranger Alex stepped outside his office. He had a serious look on his face, and his hair was all disheveled. "Everyone, if you could please gather around."

Evie, Iris, and Zak joined the crowd, making a semicircle around him.

"I understand that you have all lost things this morning," Ranger Alex said, running his hand through his hair. "Well, you're not alone. The Ranger's office has lost a few things, too. Including our walkie-talkies, our wall clock, and our power tools!"

Evie suddenly felt a little nervous. *Is there a thief in the camp? If so, maybe they took my backpack!*

"In a moment I'll be handing out forms for you to fill in," Ranger Alex went on. "So you can list everything that you've lost. I will pass them on to the police once I can call them to come investigate—only, I seem to have lost my cell, too."

Up at the front of the crowd, Evie spotted her parents. Hannah's face was pale and her shoulders were all slouchy. *She looks so sad*, Evie thought. Then she suddenly remembered how Hannah had mislaid her cell once before, and she'd been really upset . . . *Not because it was valuable*, Evie remembered her stepmom saying, *but because of all the photos of me as a toddler that were on it.* "Irreplaceable!" That was the word Hannah had used at the time. *That's why she bought the bright yellow cell phone case*, Evie thought. *So that even though the baby photos got backed up on the computer as soon as she found her cell, she knew she'd never lose it again!* Evie looked at her stepmom once more and noticed how red her eyes looked. *Has she been crying?* "Guys," Evie whispered. "We've got to find Hannah's cell."

"Yeah, and my camera," Zak said.

"And the backpack and spotter's sheet," Iris added, "or we'll never win the scavenger hunt."

"Yeah, but the cell is EXTRA important to Hannah," Evie explained. "See, Hannah takes loads of photos. And they mean a lot to her. Like when we arrived here today, did you see how she instantly got her cell out and started taking photos? Come on . . . if there is a thief in the camp, maybe we can find them and try to get her cell back." She began walking away in the other direction.

"But what about the form we need to fill in?" Zak called as he caught up with her.

"We can do that later," Evie said. "First we need to trap a thief."

Iris coughed. "And how are we going to do that?"

Evie turned back to look at her and Zak. "We just need to find someone with a really big bag of stuff."

"And a striped sweater, a ski mask, and a shirt that says 'Thief' on the front?" Iris grinned. "I don't think it'll be that easy."

"But don't forget, we've got a secret weapon," Evie said, and she bent down to hug Fudge.

CHAPTER 14

"So how exactly is Fudge going to find this thief?" Iris asked as they skirted the campsite for a second time. "I mean, he's great at licking people and wagging his tail—"

"And finding hot dogs." Zak laughed.

"And rescue princesses up trees!" Evie smiled. "But I'm sure he'll also be able to spot someone naughty."

"What, you mean, using his doggy instincts?"

Zak nodded. "Actually, that's probably true . . . I read this book once that said dogs can tell when someone is good or bad—apparently it's to do with how they smell. People who are up to no good tend to give off a whiff of nervousness."

Iris laughed. "So THAT'S why you always smell so bad."

"Hey!" Zak's face flushed.

"What else can dogs tell?" Evie asked, trying to divert the argument.

"Well, according to the book, some dogs know when you're not telling the truth."

"Oh, I can believe that," Iris said. "My cat definitely knows when I'm fibbing about there being no kitty treats left in his tin . . . But I don't think a pet could spot a thief. I mean, *we* haven't even seen any suspicious-looking people."

"Well, we've seen loads of people with backpacks," Zak said, "and the thief could have disguised themselves as a hiker."

The three friends glanced around at the campers passing by.

"I wish we had X-ray glasses," Iris whispered, peering at a young couple walking past. "Then we could see inside everyone's bags."

"But no one here looks like they are hiding anything," Evie said.

"Hey—I've thought of something," Zak said. "My mom's best friend, Bella, is a police officer, and she once told me that nine out of ten arrests are made after a neighborhood tip."

"What's that?" Iris asked.

"It's when people spot unusual things happening in their neighborhood," Zak said, "and then tell the police. So maybe we need to look at the whole campground as our neighborhood. And start watching for the person who is doing something out of the ordinary, like poking around in other people's belongings, maybe, or just hanging around, watching everyone else."

Iris chuckled. "That sounds like us!"

But Evie didn't laugh. She was checking out the groups of campers around them. Could one of them really be the thief? She watched an older lady and a man drinking coffee by their fire. *Nope, they look exactly like regular grandparents enjoying a vacation.* Then she noticed a mom walking past with a stroller. *Nah, that's not unusual. And anyway, who would take a baby with them to commit a robbery?* She turned to look in the other direction . . . *And that young couple over there are just unpacking their picnic.*

Fudge had noticed the picnic, too. He sniffed the air, then strained on his leash to get a closer look.

Iris chuckled. "I don't know about a Detective Dog . . . Fudge is more like a Snack Inspector!" But Evie was watching something else now on the other side of the campground. "Can I borrow your binoculars?" she asked Zak.

"Sure." He handed them over. "What is it?"

"That cyclist over there, in the black-and-white helmet," Evie said. "See, he's weaving in and out, around those camps . . . I saw him twice before, when we were by the Ranger's office."

"Mm, he does seem to be looking for something," Zak said.

"Let me see!" Iris took the binoculars from Evie and peered through them. "Oh wow . . . he's got a basket on the back of his bike and it's full of stuff."

"It could just be his camping equipment," Zak said. "Let me look."

"But he'd have a backpack if it was camping equipment," Iris said, passing her cousin the binoculars.

"Wait—he's stopped now," Zak said. "He's getting something out of the basket . . . now he's holding it up . . . Whoa!" Zak gasped. "NO WAY!" He lowered the binoculars and looked at the girls. "He's got a cell in his hands with a bright yellow case!"

"Huh?" Evie felt her tummy wobble. *Was it excitement? Or nervousness?* "We've got to go check it out!"

They raced across the grass, keeping their eyes

on the cyclist, who had put the cell in the basket of his bike and set off again.

"How are we going to stop him?" Zak panted. "He's going too fast."

"Football tackle?" Iris puffed. "I reckon I could take him."

"Not unless you're Superwoman!" Zak said.

"Wait!—he's stopped again," Evie said.

They slowed down to watch as the cyclist put his feet on the ground and looked around, as though he was searching for something. Then he reached into the basket and took out the yellow cell again.

"He's making a call," Zak whispered. "This is the perfect time to catch him."

"We'll need something to tie him up," Iris said. "Like a rope, maybe."

Huh? Evie gulped. "But we haven't got a rope!— Hey, Fudge, stop pulling!" Evie glanced down at the pup, who was tugging at his leash, wanting to keep moving. And suddenly, like a kick in the ankles from an annoying younger cousin, an idea popped into her head. "Um—I guess we could use Fudge's leash?"

Iris's eyes sparkled. "Brilliant! Because it's extendable, right?"

Evie nodded but she suddenly felt a little scared. *Capturing baddies isn't something I know anything about. What if he puts up a fight?*

A little nervously, she followed Iris and Zak across the grass as they stalked toward the man. Luckily, the cyclist was still on his cell and he had his head turned away from them.

"Okay, here's what we'll do," Iris whispered as they stopped a little distance away from the man. "As soon as we get closer, you stop moving," she told Evie, "and start pressing the button to release the leash. Me and Zak will run on next to Fudge and lead him in a big circle round the man, then you hit the button and the loop should tighten."

Zak frowned. "You really think this will work?"

"Sure!" Iris said. "I watch a lot of cop shows."

Evie's eyes goggled. *Do police officers really use extendable dog leashes to catch suspects?*

"Okay, let's go." Iris gave them a thumbs-up, then led the way.

As soon as they got within a few feet of the man, she nodded to Evie to press the button. Fudge, who was still zooming along, began to pull ahead, with Zak and Iris guiding him around the man in a big loop. Then Iris gave Evie a nod.

Okay, "waggy-tails crossed" this works! Evie took a deep breath and pressed the button to retract the leash . . .

It pinged back, instantly tightening around the cyclist . . .

"Hey!" he yelped. "What's going on?"

As the man spun around to look at them, they saw his face for the first time, and everyone froze.

CHAPTER 15

"Mr. Pemberton!" Iris gasped.

Evie had only seen the twins' dad once before, but there was no mistaking the resemblance. *He's got the same pointy chin*, she thought. *And the same upturned nose, the same slightly mean eyes and cranky expression . . .*

"What do you think you're doing?" Mr. Pemberton snapped, pushing the leash away from his bike. "Is this some kind of prank?"

The friends looked at one another. Then Iris coughed. "Um—sorry, Mr. Pemberton, but Evie's stepmom's cell has gone missing, and it looks awfully like the one you're holding."

Evie looked at her friend. *Whoa! You are so brave! I could never speak up like that to a grown-up.*

Mr. Pemberton's eyes bulged. "Are you accusing me of stealing? This is MY cell! Take a look at it if you don't believe me."

He held it up and Iris took a small step closer. "Er, Evie, does your stepmom's cell have a dent in the bottom left-hand corner of the case?"

"Um—I don't think so, but—"

"And does it have a scratch along the screen?" Mr. Pemberton interrupted. "A scratch that she's been meaning to fix but has been too busy working to get around to?"

"Well—I don't know . . ." Evie was starting to feel a little uneasy now. *I definitely don't remember a dent OR a scratch, but perhaps I just hadn't noticed.*

"And does your stepmom's cell . . . ," Mr.

Pemberton began. But just then it started to ring in his hand.

Uh-oh! That's definitely NOT Hannah's ringtone, Evie thought. *But maybe he changed it to cover up the fact he stole it?*

"Go ahead," Mr. Pemberton told them, waggling the ringing cell in front of them. "You can answer it if you want. It's probably my wife wondering what's happened to the hot dogs she asked me to bring up from the restaurant, on account of a bad dog stealing the ones she'd been cooking." His eyes bored into Fudge and the pup dived behind Evie's legs.

Iris glanced at the screen of the cell. "Er—it says: 'Honeybun calling'?"

Mr. Pemberton's face turned tomato red. "That's what I call my wife," he muttered, turning away from them to take the call. "Hello . . . Yes, honey, I'm here . . . I'm sorry I'm so late, but I've been cycling all around the campground because I can't find where you parked the RV . . ." He frowned at Evie.

"Yeah, I'll be there in a moment, only—I've had a bit of a holdup . . ."

Evie bit her lip. She suddenly felt about two inches tall. *I guess it really is his wife calling. And when she finds out we've accused him of being the Big Woods thief . . .* Evie's legs seemed to have turned to jelly. *On the OMG Accident Scale, this might be peaking at 11!*

Iris nudged her. "Maybe we should go now."

Evie nodded. "I am so sorry," she called to Mr. Pemberton, trying the "Apologize and Explain" technique. "It's just that your cell looks exactly like my stepmom's . . . and I've never seen anyone else with that cover before . . ."

But he'd already turned his back on them to finish his call.

"So that wasn't quite what we planned," Zak said as they walked off into the trees, as fast and as far away from Mr. Pemberton as they could get.

Evie felt her shoulders slouch.

"I guess we'd better go back to the Ranger's

office and fill in the form for our missing things," she said. "You never know, maybe someone else has caught the thief by now." *Here's hoping!*

By the time they reached the Ranger's office, most of the line outside was gone. But there were still a few people waiting to report their missing property.

Evie smiled at a little girl who was in front of them holding what looked like her dad's hand.

"I love your doggy," the little girl said. "Can I pet him?"

"Sure," Evie said, crouching down next to the pup. "This is Fudge. He loves a tickle."

"Aw, he's so cute," the girl said as Fudge's tail began to wag. "He's so soft and squishy. I wish I had a doggy."

Her dad smiled down at her. "I know, Milly, I know!" He sighed. "You tell me that all the time."

"Daddy's lost his watch," the girl whispered to Evie. "It's his new watch, so he's a bit sad."

"Oh, that's not very good," Evie said. "My friend

has lost his camera," she said, pointing to Zak. "And I can't find my backpack."

"I know where Daddy's watch has gone," the little girl said. "I told him, but he didn't listen."

Evie glanced at Zak and Iris, who were now paying attention, too.

"See, there was this pretty lady in a bright, shiny pink dress and she had a sparkly magic wand and she waved it at Daddy and his watch vanished! I saw her, Daddy, I really did."

Her father smiled wearily. "Yeah, I know, honey. But you've got THE best imagination, haven't you? Ms. Michaels always says you are the greatest storyteller in her first-grade class."

"But it's not a story, Daddy!" Milly folded her arms and pouted. "I really did see the lady AND her magic wand. She was twirling and all these sparkles were coming out of her pockets and—"

"So cute," said another camper next to them.

But Evie didn't think it sounded cute. She thought it sounded entirely believable. "Agent C!" she hissed to her friends. "She's the one stealing all the things!"

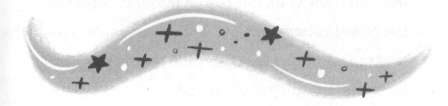

CHAPTER 16

" I just don't get it," Iris said. "Why would Agent C want to steal cell phones and watches and clocks—"

"—and power tools," Zak added.

"—and my backpack!" Evie shook her head. "I know it sounds weird, but that little girl's description fits Agent C perfectly."

They'd left the Ranger's office now and were heading back to their campsite, hoping to find Agent C on the way. But so far all they'd spotted were more cranky-looking vacationers turning their campsites upside down, searching for missing things.

"Wait! I know . . . maybe Agent C needs all the things she's taken, to turn them into something else," Evie suggested. "Like last time she visited and she tried to turn a potato into a carriage and Fudge into a horse."

At the sound of his name, the pup let out a little bark, and his tail began to wag.

"Yeah, but that didn't end well," Iris said, looking at Fudge. "Agent C turned you into a donkey, didn't she, boy."

Evie bent down and stroked the pup, making his waggy tail nearly hit a 10 on the waggy-tail-o-meter. "Don't worry, Fudge. I won't let her try that one again." She looked up at Iris and Zak. "But maybe Agent C is planning something else. Remember how she said we should lock my parents in a giant pumpkin coach?"

Zak laughed. "So, you think she's decided to use

all those cells and clocks and watches to turn them into one giant gadgety pumpkin to imprison them inside?"

"Or maybe a huge clock," Iris said. "Like Big Ben in London. My parents sent me a postcard from there. You could definitely lock your mom and dad inside Big Ben."

Zak nodded. "Though that would look so weird here in the middle of the forest."

"Hey—there she is!" Iris pointed through the trees, where a group of older people were sitting around a campfire, chatting. Behind them stood Agent C.

"Check out the sack on her back!" Zak whispered.

As the friends watched, Agent C pulled out her wand and began wafting it above the table, scattering little sparkles through the air. Instantly, the two cell phones and a clock that had been sitting there vanished, and the sack Agent C was carrying bulged out.

"Oh my word!" Evie groaned. "Agent C *is* the thief!"

The friends dashed around the back of the campsite and pounced as the agent made her escape.

"What are you doing?" Evie cried. "You can't just go around stealing stuff!"

Agent C blinked at them, her eyes wide. "But I'm not stealing anything . . ."

"Then what's that in your sack?" Zak said.

"Oh, these things . . ." Agent C's face turned pink. "I'm collecting them for safekeeping."

"Safekeeping from what?" Iris asked.

"Hannah's magical curfew!" Agent C sighed and used her wand to scratch her forehead, leaving little rainbows on her skin. "You see, I've always had to leave parties because of my magical curfew. And I don't want your stepmom to have to quit the slumber party because of hers. So I thought I'd hide all the watches, clocks, and cell phones in the camp; then she'll never find out the time, her curfew won't be broken, and she won't have to leave."

"But that's ridiculous!" Iris said.

"Oh, I agree." Agent C sighed. "Magical curfews are absolutely tiresome."

"No, I mean—"

"But don't worry," Agent C went on, "because I'm going to help Hannah beat her curfew. Did I tell you I'm in training to become a fairy godmother someday?"

The friends looked at one another.

Would Agent C make a good fairy godmother? Evie wondered. *The tale of Cinderella would definitely have been different if Agent C had been left in charge of the enchantments.*

"Perhaps I could even be *your* fairy godmother one day, Evie!" As she spoke, Agent C tapped Evie's shoulder with her wand and her clothes instantly changed color. From blue to gold. Shiny, eye-blinking, extra-sparkly, *be-able-to-see-it-from-space* sort of gold. "Oh, look at that!" Agent C breathed, admiring her own handiwork. "Sometimes I just do magic when I'm not even trying."

"Scary!" Zak muttered, taking a step backward.

Evie looked down at her shimmering pants and sweatshirt and smiled. "I kind of like them . . . though I'm not sure how I'll explain them to Hannah."

Agent C didn't hear. She was watching a man walking past who was checking his watch. "Oh, did you see that?" Agent C whispered. "Another clock . . . I'd better remove that, too."

"No! Stop!" Evie called.

But Agent C had already waggled her wand.

The man looked at his now empty wrist, then at the ground, as though he thought his watch must have somehow slipped off.

"You've got to give that back," Evie whispered to Agent C.

"Oh, I will. I'll make sure everything is returned AFTER Hannah's slumber party. Uh-oh . . . Look over there," Agent C added as a young couple pulled up in their vehicle at the campsite across the way from where they were standing. "I bet they have lots of clocks . . . I'd better go see."

"Wait!" Evie stepped in front of her. "Um—how about we carry your sack for you. It looks very heavy."

Agent C put her head to one side and sighed. "Oh, what a pet you are, Evie. If anyone deserves their own permanent fairy godmother, it is you." She slipped the sack off her shoulders and handed it over. "I'll just be a moment . . ."

"Good move," Zak whispered as Agent C trotted off. "Now everything she steals will go straight into that sack—"

"—which we can drop off at the Ranger's office!" Evie added. "But first I want to see if our things are inside." She untied the neck of the sack and rummaged inside. "There's Hannah's cell—oh, she's going to be so happy to get it back!" Evie felt a surge of positivity at the sight of it. "But I don't see the book."

"Or your backpack with our scavenger hunt things inside," Iris said, peering over Evie's shoulder. "Or your camera, Zak."

"Maybe she's stashing more stuff elsewhere?" Zak suggested. "Master criminals usually have a secret hiding place."

"Agent C is not a master criminal—" Evie began.

But she was interrupted by a shout from behind

them as Agent S jogged past, her arms full of shiny yellow fabric. "Look what I found!" she gushed. "Isn't it absolutely beautiful? Perfect for onesies. Oh, and I LOVE your party outfit, Evie. So sparkly!"

Evie looked at the little red embroidered heart that appeared above Agent S's head as she said the word *love* and smiled. She was just about to call after Agent S to tell her how much she liked the hearts when a little alarm bell sounded somewhere in the back of her mind. *Hold on . . . I'm sure I've seen the material she was carrying somewhere before . . .*

And then it came to her. "Oh no," she gasped. "It can't be!"

Iris looked at her. "What is it?"

"That fabric," Evie said. "I know who it belongs to."

But she didn't need to explain because right at that moment a familiar blond-haired figure appeared, striding across the grass, her mouth puckered like she was chewing a wasp.

"Mrs. Pemberton!" Evie squeaked.

The woman glared at them—her eyes goggling at the sight of Evie's gold outfit. "Have you seen my tablecloth? Because someone has just stolen it!"

Evie tried not to meet her gaze.

"And when I find out who . . ." Mrs. Pemberton let the unfinished sentence dangle in the air for a moment before she turned and stalked away, marching straight toward the Browns' campsite.

"Uh-oh!" Evie felt a little shiver of worry. "We need to get back to our camp, fast!"

CHAPTER 17

B ut it was already too late.

By the time Evie, Iris, and Zak reached their campsite, a volcano had erupted, and that volcano was Mrs. Pemberton!

She was glaring across the Browns' camping table at Hannah with the bundle of yellow fabric laid out between them. The twins had arrived, too. They scowled at the friends as they saw them approach. And sitting a little distance away, tucked up out of sight behind one of the tents, was Agent S, who was threading a large needle with yellow thread and singing happily to herself.

"That's my tablecloth!" Mrs. Pemberton shrieked. "Suppose you tell me how it got here."

Hannah's face was red, and her pretty scarf was pushed so far back now, it was almost falling off her hair. "As I've already told you, I've been away looking for my cell phone, so I don't know."

"First you let your dog run wild, then you take my tablecloth!" Mrs. Pemberton had her hands on her hips now, and her nostrils were flaring.

She looks like an angry bull about to headbutt Hannah! Evie thought.

"And as for the incident with my husband's bicycle . . . ," Mrs. Pemberton continued.

"What incident?" Hannah asked.

"As if you don't know!" Mrs. Pemberton exclaimed. "It's an outrage. I think your family has got a vendetta against mine."

The twins looked at each other and smirked.

"Now, wait one moment—" Hannah began.

"That tablecloth was made for me by my mother," Mrs. Pemberton interrupted. "And it's a good thing she's not here right now, because she's a lot less tolerant than me!"

"Whoa, she must be really mean then," Iris muttered.

Zak frowned. "Do you think we should go explain about the tablecloth?"

"How?" Iris whispered back. "Sorry, but Sleeping Beauty took it to turn it into a onesie for a surprise slumber party."

Evie bit her lip. *Come on, Super Chef, think of something . . . Maybe I should go make some s'mores . . . That's what worked best last summer when I went on a school camping trip and everyone squabbled over who got to sleep in which tent. Once I'd made s'mores, they all got along fine.* "Um, excuse me—" she began.

But Mrs. Pemberton just spoke over her. "If you won't apologize," she told Hannah, "then I'm going to have to ask the Ranger to call the police."

Her eyes flashed, and her face changed color from tomato red to deep-plum purple.

Evie blinked at Mrs. Pemberton, expecting steam to pop out of her ears at any moment. She glanced at her stepmom, who had suddenly gone stonily silent. *Uh-oh! I think Mrs. P has pressed Hannah's boil button!* That's what her dad always said about Hannah. She was like a slow-boiling kettle. It took her a while to get going, but once she did . . .

"I keep telling you," Hannah said through gritted teeth, "I DIDN'T TAKE YOUR TABLECLOTH!"

Just at that moment there was a shout from behind them.

"Hannah! Look!" Evie's dad appeared, waggling a box in the air, and behind him followed Ranger Alex. "We managed to borrow a tire pump— Oh, um, sorry, is something going on here?"

Both women turned to look at him. So did the twins. But that wasn't the only thing they saw.

"Oh my goodness!" Mrs. Pemberton blurted out,

gazing beyond the men to something much more shocking.

Clara let out a squeal. Katie-Belle gasped. And Hannah's eyes goggled.

"It's a . . . a . . ."

But her words were drowned out by Fudge, who had begun to tug on his leash and bark. And it wasn't his normal *Hi-I'm-Fudge-and-I-love-everyone-especially-hot-dogs* sort of a bark.

Evie spun around to see what was bothering them all. *Huh?* She did a double take. "Is that a—"

"Moose!" Zak breathed. "Awesome!"

The giant beast was lumbering past, just a few feet away from the campsite.

For a moment, all thoughts of slumber parties, tablecloths, and missing magical books seemed to evaporate as Evie gazed, spellbound, at the magnificent beast. "It-it-it's gigantic!" she breathed.

"Well, it is the largest deer in the world," Zak muttered. "And that one's got to be at least six feet

tall," he added. "And weigh a thousand pounds . . .
And did you know even bears and wolves are scared
of them and—"

"Now is not the time for 'A Hundred and One
Zak Facts' about moose!" Iris interrupted. "All I
want to know is will it get us?"

"Nah, they're really peaceful creatures," Zak said.

But as Fudge continued to bark loudly, the moose stopped and turned to look at him, tossing its enormous antlers and snorting.

"Shush, Fudge!" Evie tried to pull the pup closer. "I don't think the moose likes your woofing."

Ranger Alex stepped forward. "Everyone, keep calm," he said, his voice sounding slightly wobbly. "The moose will probably just pass on by."

WHAT TO DO IF YOU MEET A MOOSE BY RANGER ALEX

Moose are fascinating creatures and generally peaceful, but you need to give them lots of space, especially if they have calves with them. If you come across a moose, here's what to do.

1.   Back off slowly and quietly.

2. Always keep your dog on a leash; moose don't like dogs. Try to keep your dog close and quiet around a moose.

3. Don't feed a moose.

4. Never get between a moose and her calf.

5. Look out for warning signs that the moose may be about to charge: It may have its ears back, the hair on its neck may be standing on end, it may be grunting, snorting, or stomping.

6. Keep something between you and the moose—a big tree, a boulder, or a vehicle.

7. If you're in a car and a moose crosses in front of you, stop and give it time to move on. You're more likely to be injured in a vehicle collision with a moose than from a moose attack.

For more information about moose safety, check out the New Hampshire Fish and Game Department website or the National Wildlife Federation.

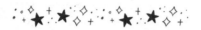

But the moose obviously hadn't got that memo. It didn't pass on by. It turned its head to get a better view of Fudge, fixing the pup with one bulging eye.

Fudge ogled the moose back, straining even harder on his leash, nearly unbalancing Evie and barking louder, as though he were shouting, *Go-away-strange-lumpy-creature-with-handlebars-on-your-head-and-leave-my-family-alone-or-I-shall-deal-with-you-puppy-style!*

Ranger Alex edged farther forward, putting himself between the moose and the group. "It's okay . . . we don't need to worry," he whispered. "Unless the moose starts grunting and stomping, and the hairs on its back start to stand up on end. Then we'll know it's about to charge—Oh dear," he mumbled, his eyes wide. "It does appear to be doing all of those things. We may need to run . . . Everyone, get ready to back off . . ."

"Oh man! I wish I had my camera!" Zak muttered.

"Me too," Iris grumbled. "We would definitely have won the scavenger hunt with a picture of a moose—hey, maybe we could borrow your stepmom's cell from the sack to take a photo?"

Evie was about to say she didn't think that was a good idea, when—

"OW!" Agent S let out a squeal. "I seem to have pricked my finger . . ."

For a moment the words didn't register with Evie—she was too busy staring at the monster moose, which was pawing the ground now. But then somewhere in the back of her brain, Agent S's words echoed in her head, and a tiny little set of warning bells began to clang . . .

Sleeping Beauty has pricked her finger? SLEEPING BEAUTY HAS PRICKED HER FINGER!!!!

Evie spun around and saw strange blue smoke—*a magical miasma!* She was sure that was what it was called in the Sleeping Beauty book she'd loved in kindergarten. It began to swirl around Agent S, and then in a heartbeat—*DONK!* The agent's head slumped forward onto the backpack she was using as a table, and suddenly she was fast asleep.

CHAPTER 18

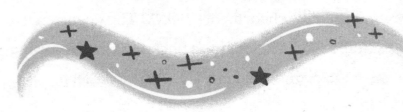

" Um—guys . . . ," Evie muttered, pointing at the swirling blue smoke, which was circling the group now.

"Oh my word!" Iris gasped. "Is that a sleeping spell?"

Zak took a step backward. "Um—we need to move—like now!"

"Wait!—shouldn't we warn them first?" Evie looked at the grown-ups, who wouldn't be able to

153

see Agent S *or* the magical mist. The twins didn't seem to have noticed what was happening, either. They were too focused on the moose, their eyes wide like pies.

Ranger Alex cleared his throat. "When I say 'run,'" he was telling everyone, "you're all going to move toward that vehicle over there and hide behind it. The moose will not charge you if you keep the vehicle between you and—" But he never finished his words. The magical miasma had reached his feet, and just like a puppet with its strings cut, he suddenly slumped to the ground, fast asleep.

The twins screamed. Mrs. Pemberton clutched her hand to her mouth.

"Ranger Alex!" she cried. But the miasma was circling her and the twins now, too, and their shoulders began to sag, and their eyes started to close. "So tired . . ." Mrs. Pemberton yawned as she crumpled onto the grass in a heap, closely followed by her daughters.

Hannah and Evie's dad were yawning, too. And

in unison, they sank into their camping chairs. In seconds, both were snoring peacefully.

Evie scooped up Fudge. "Quick!" she called to her friends. "RUN!"

Heads down, hearts thumping, the three friends charged across the grass with the miasma at their heels. As they passed other campers, Evie shouted a warning. But none of the adults could see the enchantment. And the children who did just pointed and stared, but by then it was too late, and they all quickly fell under its spell.

Evie glanced over her shoulder; people were nodding off everywhere. Some by their campfires, others propped up against the tents they were pitching. A few had even dozed off while playing Frisbee or while grilling food!

"This way!" Iris shouted, darting off down one of the trails that led into the forest. "It leads to the river. Maybe magic can't cross water."

Evie and Fudge chased after her, with Zak following.

"Faster!" he yelled. "The spell is catching up to us."

They raced down the path, diving over tree stumps and logs and swerving past prickly bushes and mud patches. They zoomed through several thick carpets of ferns, until they came to a clearing where a shallow stream bubbled past.

"Use the stepping-stones to cross it!" Iris shouted as she jumped onto the first one.

Evie scooped up Fudge and followed.

"I th-th-think we lost it," Zak panted as he joined them on the other side of the water. He peered back the way they'd come, searching for the blue smoke. "I don't see it now; maybe you're right, Iris, magic can't cross water."

"That was so freaky," Iris puffed as she collapsed on a large rock. "I was sure it was going to get us."

"Me too!" Evie knelt by the stream and splashed water on her face, while Fudge had a drink. She leaned back on her heels, still trying to catch her breath. She was just about to ask what they should do next, when suddenly her eyes were drawn to the trees, back the way they'd come. "Hey—are those branches moving?"

Her friends looked where she was looking.

"They're not moving," Zak said. "They're grow-ing!"

As they watched, large leaves the size of dinner plates sprouted from nowhere, while new shrubs shot out of the ground and the trunks of the trees began to groan as they stretched and extended.

Iris jumped to her feet. "I know what this is! In the Sleeping Beauty story, a thick forest grows around the castle—"

"—and cuts it off for a hundred years!" Evie gasped. "I'm not going to see my parents for a century!" She felt her legs turn to spaghetti. "Come on, we've got to get back inside that forest before the trees block us out forever." She tugged Fudge's leash and jumped back across the stepping-stones over the water.

"But if we go back in, won't we fall asleep?" Zak asked as he followed behind.

"I don't think so," Evie said. "The blue smoke has gone now." But she wasn't sure. From what she was learning, magic never quite behaved like it was supposed to do in fairy tales.

"Ugh, these branches are too tight," Iris groaned as they tried to push their way back through the trees.

"And spiky!" Zak added, catching his shirt on one of the thorns.

"Look! Fudge has found a gap . . ." Evie dropped to her hands and knees and crawled through the foliage behind the pup.

Iris and Zak wriggled through after her. Just in time . . .

"It's gone!" Zak glanced back over his shoulder and watched the hole they'd just passed through vanish, filled up already with dark leaves and branches and thick brambles. "So I guess we're stuck in here now."

"Hopefully not for a hundred years," Iris said. "Because that would be WAY too much of you, Zak."

"One hundred milliseconds is too much with you!" he snapped back.

"Guys!" Evie held up her hands to stop the argument before it got worse. "We need to think about what we're going to do now. The whole camp is asleep!" Evie puffed out her cheeks. "I can't believe we're actually in the middle of a fairy tale."

Zak grunted. "I hate fairy tales!"

Evie had always liked the idea of being a character in a storybook. But now that she was actually living in one, she wasn't so sure. *What if I can't wake my parents again? What if none of us can ever escape from here? How am I going to become a world-famous super chef, writing cookbooks and hosting my own baking channel?* She gritted her teeth. *Come on, Super Chef, good bakers don't give in that easy. This is just like the time when you entered the school bake-off and you couldn't figure out why your sponge cake kept sagging in the middle, and you had to try lots of things to find out what was happening until eventually you discovered it was because Hannah kept opening the oven door* to take a peek to make sure it wasn't burning. "Don't worry," Evie told Zak. "I'm sure there must be some way to break the spell."

Iris's eyes sparkled with mischief. "There is. Beauty will need a kiss from a handsome prince. But since we haven't got one of them—" She looked at her cousin.

"What?" Zak's face turned pale. "NO WAY!"

CHAPTER 19

" I told you!" Zak said, shooting a scowl at his cousin. "I am NOT kissing anyone!"

After pushing their way through the rest of the fast-growing magical forest wall, they'd made it back to the campground trail, passing several snoozing campers on the way. But so far they hadn't come up with another solution to the problem of the Sleeping Beauty spell.

"We'll probably be stuck here forever, then," Iris grumbled. She bent down to stroke Fudge, who was trotting by their feet. "Maybe we should get you to do the kissing instead. You're WAY more of a handsome prince than Zak, aren't you?" The pup jumped up and licked her cheek. "Ha! Exactly like that, right, Evie?"

But Evie wasn't paying attention. She was staring at something on the path in front of her. "A pine cone . . . ," she breathed, picking it up and turning it over in her hand. She looked up at Iris and Zak. Then—"Of course!" she blurted out. "What if Sleeping Beauty doesn't actually need a kiss to wake her up?"

"But that's what always happens in the Sleeping Beauty story," Iris said.

"What if this time it isn't," Evie said. "Maybe *our* Sleeping Beauty has a different story." Evie held up the pine cone. "Remember Agent R told us it was going to rain, because that pine cone she found was all closed up, just like this one."

"Sure, but what's that got to do with the Sleeping Beauty spell?" Zak asked.

"Nothing, apart from telling us that the stories in our magical fairy-tale book aren't always the ones we've read before. I mean, did you know Agent R was a weather forecaster?"

Iris cocked her head to one side. "No, but—"

"And none of us knew that Sleeping Beauty likes making clothes out of recycled fabric," Evie went on. "And that she enjoys collecting recipes with her friend the Very Useful Prince and throwing slumber parties and—"

"Making onesies!" Zak shuddered. "You're right! We didn't know that. And don't forget the other Beauty we met before . . . She told us she used to be a librarian for animals, and that wasn't in any of the Beauty and the Beast stories."

Iris nodded slowly. "Yeah, I get that. So you think our Sleeping Beauty might have a different ending to her story?"

"Exactly!" Evie said. "See, I didn't actually read any of the fairy tales in the magical book, did you guys?"

Iris and Zak both shook their heads.

"I wish I had," Iris said. "Because, are you forgetting, we've LOST the book. So we have no idea what happens in Agent S's story."

Evie grimaced. "Yeah, that is a problem. Somehow we've got to find the book."

"But it could be anywhere." Iris looked around at the different tents and RVs dotted all over the campground. "If Agent C didn't take it, someone else must have."

"Maybe Fudge could find it," Zak suggested.

Iris chuckled. "He didn't do very well last time we tried to get him to find stuff."

"But he did find Agent R," Evie said.

"And the Pembertons' hot dogs!" Zak grinned. "So he can smell stuff. We just need to help him to know exactly what he's looking for. Remember

I told you I read a magazine article about sniffer dogs? Well, they always started by giving the dogs a scent to follow."

Evie's eyes sparkled. "Oh yeah, I saw a TV show about a dog that found a missing hiker. They gave it an old sock the man had left in his tent, so the dog could recognize his scent."

"But we haven't got anything that smells of old magical fairy-tale book," Iris said.

"We've got me!" Evie said. "And it's my backpack we need to find. So if we can get Fudge to smell something of mine, like—um—this sweatshirt!" She tugged the shiny gold top off over her head and dangled it out in front of the pup. "Then it might work, right, Zak?"

"Sure . . . hold it closer to his nose. Make sure he gets a really good sniff."

As Evie thrust the sweatshirt toward the pup, he made a lunge for it.

"Hey!" Evie giggled. "You're not supposed to eat

it!" She managed to wrestle it out of his mouth and rubbed it gently on his nose. "Do you really think this will work?" she asked Zak.

He shrugged. "It's better than the kissing option."

Iris giggled. And Evie tried to hide a smile.

"Okay then, let's try it." Evie unhooked the pup's leash from his collar and gave him a quick hug. "Go on, Fudge . . . Find my backpack!"

For a moment, the pup just stood there, as though he couldn't quite believe he was actually being allowed off the leash. Then he shook himself all over, gave a single excited bark, and ran off.

CHAPTER 20

Following a puppy is not easy, Evie decided as she scratched her leg on the hollow log that Fudge was currently torpedoing through. *He seems to think I can do all the stuff he can. Only he's got fur. And I just have skin!*

They'd been chasing after Fudge for at least ten minutes now. And so far, all he'd found were two old candy wrappers, a pile of wildlife poop (Zak said it was from a fox), and one cranky squirrel that definitely didn't want to be the pup's friend.

"We're going around in circles," Iris puffed. "I'm sure we've seen that old couple snoozing on their blow-up chairs three times already."

"I think there are just a lot of older people asleep on blow-up chairs," Evie said, though she was trying not to look too closely at all the fast-asleep campers they passed. *It's like being in a giant wax museum*, she thought. *And they always give me the creeps.* "Hey—Fudge!" she called as the pup stopped to sniff out a trash can. "You've got to find the backpack, not a snack pack!"

"Maybe we need to give him another whiff of your sweatshirt," Zak suggested.

But just then the pup turned, sniffed the air, and zoomed off in the other direction.

Please let him find the backpack this time, Evie thought, *otherwise we're never going to break the spell!* And she didn't want to imagine what that might mean.

Fudge was running faster now, darting through more spiky bushes, across a muddy ditch, and around a row of thick pine trees, before breaking out of the trees and arriving in another campsite where he began barking wildly.

"He's found something!" Evie panted as she followed him into the camp, but then—"Oh no!" She looked around at the fancy RV, the bicycle propped up against it, with the black-and-white helmet resting on the top and the four chairs—two of them pink with the letters *C* and *KB* embroidered on them. She looked at the table, too, which last time Evie had seen it, had had a bright yellow tablecloth on it, but now had two puppy paws instead, as Fudge helped himself to a fresh plate of hot dogs sitting there.

"Not this place again!" Iris panted as she and Zak arrived at Evie's side. "You're lucky the Pembertons aren't here, Fudge, or Mrs. P would be making herself a pair of puppy slippers out of you by now."

"Hey—I wonder where *Mr.* Pemberton is," Zak whispered, as though the twins' dad might hear them. "Because he wasn't over by our campsite, so I guess he must be here somewhere." Zak crept over to the RV window and peeped inside. "There he is! Fast asleep on the couch."

Evie moved the plate of hot dogs out of the pup's reach and sighed. "So much for Fudge finding my backpack."

"Wait a minute . . ." Zak was squinting at something by his feet. He bent down and reached behind one of the front tires of the RV.

"My backpack!" Evie squealed, so loud that Fudge jumped. She took it from Zak, quickly opened the top, and looked inside. "Oh thank goodness," she breathed as she pulled out the magical book. She clutched it to her chest and felt a wave of relief pass over her. "But I don't understand. How did it get here?"

"I think I can guess," Iris said, her eyes narrowing. "Remember who was hanging around that part of the forest just before you lost it . . ."

"The twins!" Evie shook her head. "They are

so sneaky." Evie didn't want to think about what might have happened if Katie-Belle or Clara had discovered the magical book . . . She shuddered. *I must never let it out of my sight again!*

"And you know, I bet they loosened Fudge's leash, too, just before he ran off to find Agent R. Remember how Katie-Belle was touching the leash when you'd tied it to the tree?" Iris frowned. "We're going to have to come up with a really awful forfeit for the twins to do when they lose the scavenger hunt."

"Um—hello!" Zak said. "Have you forgotten the small matter of the sleeping spell we've still got to break?"

"Well, if you'd been a handsome prince, we'd have done that ages ago."

"Pax, pax!" Evie said, stepping in between them to stop the argument. She had learned that *pax* was the word Gammy always made the cousins say whenever they argued. Apparently, it was Latin for *peace*. She rummaged inside the backpack again and pulled out Zak's camera . . . "Here," she said, handing it to him. ". . . And the spotting sheet . . ." She gave that to Iris. Then she dropped her backpack on the floor and held up the magical book. "Now, let's find out what really happened in Agent S's story." *And fingers crossed we don't actually need a handsome prince!*

CHAPTER 21

ONCE UPON A THIMBLE, in a land far away, lived a princess who loved sewing. Clothes. Toys. Blankets. Drapery! The princess could turn her hand to anything.

She was particularly clever at reusing old fabric. She'd scour the kingdom looking for unwanted clothes to turn into beautiful new creations.

One bright, sunny August, it was the princess's birthday and she decided to hold a huge slumber party under the stars, on the castle grounds. Everyone was invited!

But the princess was so busy getting everything ready for her party . . . sewing onesies and garlands and napkins and decorations . . . she forgot to send a few of the invitations.

One of those whose invitation didn't arrive was a cranky young fairy named Amanita.

When she found out about the party, Amanita was so angry, she decided to punish the princess. She went to the castle with a gift. But no one knew she had put a wicked enchantment on it.

When the princess unwrapped the present, she found a beautiful sewing box shaped like a swan, which was full of needles and pins and threads. The princess loved it and said she couldn't wait to use it.

"Oh," said Amanita, "then perhaps you could repair this little tear in my frock?"

The princess was happy to help. But when she began to sew, she pricked her finger on the needle and immediately fell into a deep, deep sleep. And so did all the guests at the party . . .

Then a thick forest grew around the castle.

The other fairies, who weren't affected by the magic, asked Amanita to reverse the spell. But she

wouldn't. She told them the enchantment would last for a hundred years.

The fairies couldn't wake the princess, but they could add an enchantment of their own . . . They knew that the only thing that could break the spell was something as powerful as love. So they cast a spell with a little red embroidered heart. If someone came to the castle who loved their hobby as much as the princess had loved sewing, then the enchantment would be broken, and she would wake up.

People came from far and wide to try to break the spell. But none of them were as passionate about their hobbies as the princess.

Years later, a Very Useful Prince came foraging. He was looking for interesting herbs and fungi to use in his hobby, which was cooking. The prince loved cooking and he was very good at it.

He hacked his way through the forest and discovered the princess fast asleep in the castle garden. He tried to wake her up. But she didn't stir.

Tired from his journey, he decided to camp there for the night before he returned home. He lit a fire and began to cook. Soon, delicious cooking smells drifted through the castle grounds and the princess's nose began to twitch. Her tummy started to rumble. And then she woke up! And so did everyone else in the castle.

The prince's passion for cooking had broken the spell!

Of course, the princess and the Very Useful Prince lived happily ever after . . . enjoying their individual hobbies even more than before!

CHAPTER 22

Evie shut the book with a triumphant *snap!* "YES!" she said. "The story really was different."

Zak grinned. "And now I definitely don't need to kiss anyone. Awesome!"

"But I don't see how this helps," Iris said. "How are we going to find the prince to come cook for her?"

"We don't need the prince," Evie said. "I can cook for Agent S."

Iris blinked at her friend. "Oh yeah! I forgot. You love making desserts."

"And s'mores smell *soooo* delicious when they're cooking," Evie said. "They're sure to wake her up." Evie slid the book into her backpack. "This Sleeping Beauty story makes so much more sense than the ones I've read before . . . Whenever Dad makes his super-special peach pancakes, me and Hannah always wake up."

"Apple pie does the same thing for me," Zak added.

"For breakfast?" Evie giggled.

Zak shrugged. "Any time is apple pie time! And it's a million times better than a kiss. No one would ever bother getting out of bed for one of those."

Evie grinned. "Come on, let's get back to the camp and get started."

As they ran back along the path, Evie noticed the forest felt so different under the sleeping spell. *It's too quiet,* she thought, glancing up at the trees. *No birdsong or animal noises. Or people calling to one another . . .*

Iris had noticed, too. "It's like a zombie apocalypse!"

"Well, let's hope none of the campers start sleepwalking," Zak muttered. "Because then I'll be OUT of this forest ASAP!"

Back at the camp, everything was exactly as they had left it. Evie's parents were dozing in their camping chairs. Ranger Alex was fast asleep on his back, snoring loudly. And Mrs. Pemberton was curled up on the ground with the twins by her side. Agent S was in a deep sleep, too, with her head still resting on the backpack she'd been sitting next to.

"It feels so weird," Evie whispered. "Like we should tiptoe around them, in case we wake them all up, when that's exactly what we want to do."

"Look!" Iris said. "The moose is still here. I wondered if the spell would work on him."

As they walked over to take a look, Fudge growled a little. But the creature was napping peacefully, its huge antlers poking up in the air.

"Maybe I could get a photo of it now?" Zak

suggested. "There's no way I'd dare to get this close when it's awake."

The moose suddenly snuffled in its sleep and Evie jumped back, while Fudge dived behind her legs. "It looks like it could wake up at any moment! Come on, I'd better go get the ingredients ready for my s'mores."

"So what do you put in them?" Iris asked, following her over to the food storage box.

Before Evie could reply, a tiny insect buzzed past her nose. "Hey!" She wafted it away, but it zoomed straight back again.

"What is that?" Iris asked. "It looks like it's glowing!"

"Maybe it's a UFO?" Zak called over.

Iris chuckled. "Aliens landing here today would not surprise me."

But just then the bug seemed to explode and—

"Agent C!" Evie gasped as the agent appeared before them.

"Oh, there you all are!" she said, doing a quick spin on the spot. "I'm so glad you didn't get sucked into that silly sleeping spell." Agent C stretched out her arms and neck for a moment and did a quick leg bend. "Ugh, I always get stiff when I'm that small."

"What was that thing?" Evie asked.

"Oh, you mean the twinkly-winkly flying bead?" Agent C smiled proudly. "It's just a little enchantment my FG taught me. It's very handy when Agent S is around. She's always pricking her finger and making everyone fall asleep. But when I'm a tiny sparkle, I can dodge the spell."

"That's not the only way to avoid it!" came another voice.

Evie spun around to find Rapunzel striding toward them, her long, silvery locks billowing in the breeze.

"If you've got a good set of lungs, you can blow any enchantment away! Look, I'll show you . . ." Agent R put her hands on her hips, took a deep breath, and blew out a giant blast of air, which made Evie's hair swish. "Deep-sea diver's lungs!" Agent R said proudly, puffing out her chest.

Agent C glanced around at the sleeping people. "So I'm guessing we're waiting for the prince to show up to break the spell . . ."

Agent R snorted. "You'll be waiting a long time. He can never tear himself away from his kitchen."

"I was thinking that maybe I could wake the princess," Evie said. "With my special s'mores?"

The agents looked at each other.

"I like it!" Agent R said, her eyes shining. "When I was a waitress, I was always having to think fast and solve my own problems. Like that time when Goldilocks tried to leave my restaurant without paying"—Agent R's eyes narrowed—"she is always wanting a free meal. But I had her back on her chair, and her wallet out, before you could say 'Porridge!'"

Evie gulped. Agent R had mentioned once before that she had been a waitress. But the thought of her as a server was pretty terrifying. *I hope she never wants to work in my parents' diner!*

"Well, you'd better get cooking," Agent C told Evie. "Because we've also got a party to plan."

Agent R grunted. "I told you, that's not going to happen . . . it's going to rain."

"Poppycock!" Agent C said. "Now, there's lots to do, so everyone will have to help."

"Not me." Agent R folded her arms. "I'm busy working on my own project. I only came back to return Ranger Alex's power tools to his office."

Evie glanced at Iris and Zak. *So that's who took Alex's tools! But why did she need them?*

Zak leaned in closer to Evie and Iris. "I hope she's not still planning to build that tower."

"What did you say?" Agent R's eyes bored into him.

"He said he really needs to go take a shower!" Evie said. "Because he slipped in fox poop, right, Zak?"

"Um—yeah, I guess," he said.

"And I've just spotted something else you need to do . . ." Agent C picked up the sack of cell phones and watches and clocks from where Evie had dumped it earlier when the moose had appeared. "You need to go hide this so Hannah's magical curfew doesn't cause a problem when everyone wakes up."

"Oh yeah, sure," Zak said, taking the sack from her. "I'll go hide it." Then he mouthed, "In the Ranger's office!" to Evie and Iris when Agent C wasn't looking.

"And maybe I should take this back," Iris said, scooping up the Pembertons' tablecloth. "So when

Mrs. P wakes up, she'll have nothing to grumble about."

"Great idea! And take some of these, too." Evie opened the food box and pulled out some of their hot dogs. "To make up for all their hot dogs that Fudge ate."

"Keep your camera handy," Iris told Zak as they headed off. "Maybe we can try to pick up some more photos for the scavenger hunt on the way."

Evie felt a wave of excitement. *Everything is starting to work out.* She bent down and tickled Fudge's ears. *Now all I need to do is make sure I cook up THE best s'mores ever; good enough to break the sleeping spell.*

CHAPTER 23

Agent R looked at the dustcloth Agent C was waggling in front of her and let out a growl. "I told you. I haven't got time to clean up the camp."

"Nonsense. We can't have a party unless the campsite is as clean as a new pin."

Evie, who was laying out the ingredients for the s'mores, wondered if she should explain that a campsite was never spotless, which was one of the things that made it special. *But if cleaning the camp keeps the agents busy, maybe I should just let them get on with it.*

"Haven't you got a better job for me to do?" Agent R moaned, flicking the dustcloth half-heartedly at the tents.

"Well, you could move the moose, I suppose," Agent C said. "He's in the way."

Evie gasped. "You can't move a moose!"

"Sure I can." Agent R flexed her muscles. "I once shifted an elephant out of a rowboat—but that's another story."

Evie gaped. *An elephant? Out of a rowboat?*

Agent R marched over to where the moose was snoozing. She bent down and peered at it. Then she walked all the way around it and back again, before declaring: "No problem!" Next she did a few arm stretches and shoulder shrugs. Then she rolled up the sleeves of her frock, spat on her hands—"For grip!" she explained—and bent down and scooped it up.

"Whoa!" Evie's eyes goggled. "How on earth—"

"Oh, she's always showing off like that," Agent

C said, not looking up from the logs she was adding to the campfire.

Evie watched as Agent R staggered off with the moose, heading out of camp. "Hey—where are you taking it?"

"The woods!" Agent R grunted.

Agent C let out a low *hurrumph!* sound. "That's just so she can get out of helping clean up the camp. She probably won't even come back. But don't worry . . . ," she said, looking at Evie, her eyes suddenly sparkly and excited, "because I've just thought of a brilliant idea."

"You have?" Evie smiled nervously. Agent C's ideas weren't always as brilliant as she thought they were.

"You see, we're going to need help with the party," Agent C said. "So I think we'd better get some more agents to lend a wand."

Now, that IS a brilliant idea! "Are you going to call on more agents from the book?" Evie imagined who might pop out of the magical fairy-tale book next . . . *Snow White, maybe. Or the Little Mermaid—* Evie loved her story. *Or perhaps the Frog Princess, or maybe even Beauty from "Beauty and the Beast" . . . I hope it's her again,* Evie thought, *because last time she came, she gave me Fudge, and she's so kind and lovely and—*

"Oh no, no!" Agent C said. "Most of the agents are very unhelpful, so many silly ideas. We just need more of me."

Evie frowned. "But how—"

"I'm going to do a multiplication spell," Agent C said, turning her magic wand toward herself. "Ten of me to do ten times the work ten times faster!"

And before Evie could stop her, Agent C waggled the wand and tapped it nine times against her chest.

CHAPTER 24

There was a flash of gold and the faint scent of pineapple, then Agent C began to expand . . .

Like life-size paper dolls! Evie thought as more and more Agent Cs appeared, each identical to the last, all standing in one long line, holding hands.

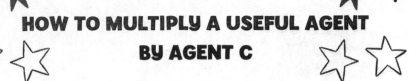

HOW TO MULTIPLY A USEFUL AGENT BY AGENT C

If only there were lots of me—I'd get so much more magic done! That's why I invented the Agent C multiplication spell. But don't worry. You don't need to be an Agent of H.E.A.R.T. to make lots of useful rescue princesses. Try folding your own helpful team!

You will need:

- A rectangle of paper (an 8.5 x 11 inch piece of printer paper works well)

- Pens or pencils to decorate

How to make:

- Fold the rectangle in half. Then turn the folded paper sideways and fold it in half again. Turn and fold one more time.

- Draw a picture of me on your folded rectangle.

- Make sure my arms and the corners of my dress extend all the way to the edges and seem to continue off the page, like in the drawing here.

- With the paper still folded, cut out your drawing of me, but don't cut along the edges where my hands or the corners of my dress would be.

- Unfold and decorate! I love pink, by the way.

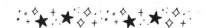

It was too much for Fudge. He dived into Evie's tent, refusing to come out.

Not that the Agent Cs seemed to notice. They had begun to sway and swing their arms, then they launched into a rousing chant . . .

One, two: The fairy-tale crew!

Three, four: Bring on the chores!

Five, six: We've got lots of tricks!

Seven, eight: We'll get things all straight!

Nine, ten: Let's sing this again.

And they did! Over and over again. And suddenly the camp was a swirl of activity—and magic sparkles!—as the Agents Cs got to work.

"You help Evie with the cooking," the original Agent C called to two of the others. "Because I'm sure her parents wouldn't want her cooking on the open fire without supervision."

Actually, that's probably true, Evie thought, handing them the toasting forks for the marshmallows.

"And everyone else," the original Agent C called, "clean up and make the camp look pretty!"

Evie watched as some of the agents dusted and swept and sorted and tidied (stepping around the sleeping campers as they worked), while others mag-ic-ed up fresh posies of flowers and strings of fairy lights that they threaded around the tents, and hung pretty lanterns around the trees surrounding the camp. Another agent found the fabric garlands that Agent S had left in the tent, along with several green satin cushions, matching chair covers, and some cozy throws that looked perfect for a night under the stars.

Meanwhile two other agents dressed the table with flowers and colorful glasses and plates, and a shiny blue tablecloth with gold twinkly bits. Another conjured up some soft, tinkling wind chimes, which she hung on the tents.

And the agents who were helping with the cook-ing didn't just toast the s'mores. They rolled up their frock sleeves and set about laying out loads of the other food that Evie had brought with her, too—sal-ads, pasta, breads and sauces and desserts, while Evie got to work on the delicious fillings for her s'mores.

EVIE BROWN'S SUPER-DUPER S'MORES RECIPES

I love making s'mores because they include a lot of my favorite ingredients: marshmallows, chocolate, and graham crackers! But the best thing about them is experimenting with extra ingredients. Here's how to make a basic s'more, plus a few of my other top flavor combinations.

Basic s'mores recipe

Ingredients:

- Graham crackers

- Squares of chocolate

- Marshmallows

- Wooden toasting sticks

- A campfire

Method:

- Break a graham cracker in half and lay on a plate. (You will use one half for the bottom of the s'more and one for the top.)

- Add two squares of chocolate to cover one half of the cracker.

- Using a stick, toast a marshmallow on the campfire, turning it around until the marshmallow becomes light golden brown on the outside and soft in the middle (approximately a minute or so).

- Add the marshmallow to the graham cracker and chocolate.

- Top with the other half of the graham cracker. Squish together and enjoy!

Ice cream s'mores

Add a scoop of vanilla ice cream onto your traditional s'more. It's super cool!

Banana surprise s'mores

Split a banana open and add in your basic s'mores ingredients. Wrap it all up in foil. Then place on your campfire for a few minutes until it's all melted and gooey.

Cookie s'mores

Replace the graham crackers with your favorite cookies! I think chocolate chip works the best.

Peach & chocolate s'mores

Fresh peach slices, marshmallow, and small squares of dark chocolate are delicious together. (These are my dad's favorite s'mores.)

Popcorn s'mores

Make a batch of popcorn, drizzle with maple syrup, then make your basic s'mores and serve all together in a bowl. Yum-tastic!

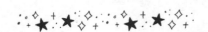

The marshmallows hadn't been toasting long when Iris and Zak got back.

"Wait until you see the photos we got," Iris called. "We found this awesome bird's nest, and a cobweb the same size as Fudge, and beetles and a caterpillar and this beautiful butterfly and—" She suddenly stopped talking and her mouth hung open as she noticed the army of Agent Cs.

Zak had seen them, too. "This is worse than a zombie apocalypse!"

Evie grinned. "It's actually quite helpful. Look how lovely the camp looks now."

Iris and Zak somehow managed to tear their eyes away from all the Agent Cs and gazed around them.

"It does look amazing," Iris said.

Zak nodded. "Now all we need to do is wake everyone up."

Evie's shoulders drooped a little. The s'mores had been ready for a few minutes, and so far, no one in the camp had stirred.

Evie took a plate of them closer to where Agent S was snoozing. She wafted the warm marshmallow under the agent's nose.

"Maybe she doesn't like s'mores," Iris said. "My mom says they're a little too sweet."

"Perhaps I should make more popcorn," Evie suggested. "She liked that earlier— Wait—" She sat back on her heels and looked up to the sky. "Did you hear that thunder?"

"Nooo!" Iris wailed. "Agent R said it was going to rain."

"That's not thunder," Zak said. "It's Agent S's tummy rumbling."

They all looked at the princess and saw her nose was twitching now, too. Then suddenly her eyes popped open, and she licked her lips. "Mmm," she breathed. "S'mores! I LOVE s'mores." And a tiny embroidered red heart shape appeared above her head.

CHAPTER 25

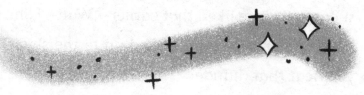

Agent S was soon tucking in, dribbling melted marshmallow and chocolate down her chin. "Oooh, delicious!" she mumbled between mouthfuls.

As she chomped and chewed her way through the plate, the rest of the camp began to stir, too. Ranger Alex was first. For a second he didn't seem to know where he was, but as he got to his feet, his eyes darted to the edge of the campsite. "The moose . . . ," he began.

"Oh, it headed off into the woods ages ago," Evie said.

"It did?" Ranger Alex frowned. "But I thought—"

"You always say how shy moose are," Zak interrupted.

"That's true but—"

He was drowned out by a giant yawning noise from Evie's dad. The others were stirring now, too. They stretched and scratched and looked around as though they couldn't quite remember where they were or what they'd been doing before the spell had struck.

Evie glanced at the twins, who were on their feet now, too, blinking in the bright sunshine. *I hope they don't say anything when they spot the Agents of H.E.A.R.T. . . .* But as she checked to see what the agents were doing, she noticed Beauty had her head down, rummaging in her backpack while the team of Agent Cs seemed to have wandered off.

"I think they're fetching firewood," Iris whispered. "See, over there . . ." She pointed to the trees, where ten pink frocks could be seen disappearing into the woods.

Just then they heard another yawn. And they both turned to look at Evie's stepmom, who was rubbing her eyes and stretching.

Evie wondered what Hannah's reaction would be when she saw the spruced-up campsite. *Will she change her mind about leaving? Please let her decide to stay.*

But before Hannah could notice anything, Mrs. Pemberton cleared her throat. She seemed to realize that she had been in the middle of something, but she obviously couldn't quite remember what it was, and then suddenly she did! Her face clouded over, and she looked down at the table, her mouth opening as though she was about to shout about her precious tablecloth—

But it wasn't there. Iris and Zak had already returned it. Instead, the table was laid out for Hannah's slumber party.

"Goodness!" Hannah breathed, suddenly spotting the table and the flowers and the food and the decorations . . . Then she noticed Evie and her golden outfit. "W-w-what happened here?"

"Surprise!" Evie said, her voice sounding slightly wobbly. "We're having a slumber party!"

"Um—yeah—" Iris said. "We planned the party while you were off looking for your cell."

"Which is here!" Zak said, holding the yellow cell phone out to her. "We—er—found it for you."

Hannah took the cell, unable to stop looking around her. "Um—thank you," she said, her voice a mixture of gratitude and confusion. "But I don't understand—"

At the sound of Hannah's voice, Fudge poked his head out of the tent flap and dived out with a *Hello-Hannah-I'm-so-glad-you-are-back-because-nothing-strange-ever-happens-when-you're-around* sort of a bark. And he ran over to her, wagging his tail.

"Ugh!" Mrs. Pemberton cried as she laid eyes on Fudge. "That dog again!" She turned away. "Come on, girls, let's get back to our camp."

"I really can't believe how amazing it all looks," Evie's dad said as the Pembertons stalked past him. "Where did you get all the cups and plates and flowers and blankets and—and those clothes, Evie!"

"A friend lent them to us," Iris said.

Which was kind of true.

"Well, I think it's a wonderful surprise, don't you, Hannah?"

"I do, of course . . . only, we were about to pack up. And I told Dawn at the pet shelter that we'd be there before it gets dark."

"Oh, you can't miss the judging for the scavenger hunt," Ranger Alex said. "There's a big box of camping goodies up for grabs."

"Please, Hannah!" Evie gave her stepmom her most desperate pleading face. "Just a little longer."

"I'm sure that'll be fine, won't it, honey?" Evie's

dad smiled at Hannah. "After all the work the kids have done . . ."

Hannah nodded. "Sure. You kids go join in the judging. And good luck!"

Evie's dad reached for the coffeepot. "And I'll fix us a hot drink . . . my throat feels so dry, it's almost as though I've been asleep for a hundred years."

The friends looked at one another and tried not to laugh.

"You can leave Fudge with us," Evie's dad added. "I'm sure he's had enough excitement for one day."

He winked at Evie, and she felt a sudden surge of hope. *Dad looks like he wants to stay . . . Maybe the slumber party plan really is going to work!*

CHAPTER 26

"Your s'mores are bound to win the contest," Iris said as she led the way over to the Ranger's office, clutching one that was wrapped in foil.

"Lucky you remembered camp food was on the list!" Zak said.

Evie nodded. But her brain was abuzz. "Guys . . . do you think Hannah will change her mind about leaving?"

"Well, she looked awfully comfy in her chair when we left the camp," Iris said.

"And your dad didn't look like he wanted to leave anytime soon," Zak added. "Remember Alex gave him a tire pump, but I didn't see him go and use it."

"That's true!" Evie tried to contain the surge of excitement she was feeling. She lifted her chin and breathed in the scent of the pine trees around her. And then she heard tweeting, too. "Oh, it's so good to hear the sound of birds again. I really don't want to go home now."

"Hey—look!" Zak pointed ahead, where the twins were marching toward the Ranger's office. "They're going to get such a shock when they see we got all our things back!"

By the time they arrived at the cabin, there were already dozens of kids—and a few parents—waiting for the judging. At the front of the room, Evie could see Alex with a round-faced lady wearing the same uniform as his, but with more badges on the front. *The Head Ranger?* Evie wondered. They were looking through Agent C's sack of cells and clocks and watches that Zak and Iris had secretly dropped off there earlier.

"I don't understand it . . . ," Evie could hear Ranger Alex saying. "Who would take all of these things, then return them?"

The Head Ranger shrugged. "Perhaps it was a prank. Or maybe someone had a change of heart. Whatever the reason, I'm glad we can give them back. And now we'd better sort out our scavengers!" She turned and smiled at the kids in the office. "Okay, everyone, come show us what you found!"

The little kids went first.

They revealed large collections of interesting objects. Some they'd brought with them. Others they'd drawn. And there were lots of pictures on their cameras, too. While Ranger Alex checked each team's sheet to see how many items they'd managed to find, the Head Ranger looked at the extra-special items that the competitors were most proud of.

"Extra points if you impress me!" she told them. "And it takes a lot to do that."

"Whoa, check out that otter print!" Zak said, peering at the drawing a little girl was holding up. "She's copied the webbing between the toes so well. Oh—and look at that boy's long-horned beetle!"

Iris laughed. "I'm not sure he was supposed to actually bring the beetle into the office!"

There were loads of other exciting finds, too. A photo of a bright blue butterfly, which the Head Ranger said was quite rare. A drawing of a giant clump of red-capped mushrooms, which Evie thought looked exactly like the sort of place a family of fairies might live inside. And loads of colorful feathers, including a black-and-white one, which belonged to a woodpecker.

And then it was their turn.

Iris stepped forward, but the Pembertons pushed in front of her.

"Look at this awesome cobweb we found!" Clara said, putting her camera so close to the Head Ranger it nearly touched her nose.

"And we actually got a picture of the spider that made it, too!" Katie-Belle added. "See? It's sitting there eating that bug it's caught."

"That is impressive," the Head Ranger said, looking at it closely. "I think it's an orb weaver spider."

Iris looked at Zak and Evie. Their cobweb photo didn't have a spider in the picture. "Um—we've got a really pretty butterfly," Iris said, showing Zak's camera screen to the ranger.

"A tortoiseshell, I think," Zak added.

"Good identification." The Head Ranger smiled at him. "Extra points for recognizing your own finds."

"Well, our mom says this is a painted lady butterfly," Clara said, shoving their camera in front of Zak's. "And it looks bigger than their butterfly. AND we got a photo of a real chrysalis hanging on a branch."

And so it went on . . . every time Iris showed the judge something good, the twins tried to better it.

"Look, Mrs. Ranger," Katie-Belle said, pushing their camera in front of her again. "We took our tree selfie dangling upside down from the branches."

The Head Ranger chuckled. "That's definitely the most creative pose I've seen so far."

"We go to gymnastics," Clara said proudly.

Iris looked at their tree selfie on the camera screen. "Um—ours is just the regular way up."

"But extra points for the dog in the picture," the Head Ranger said, her eyes twinkling. "I love dogs. What sort is—"

"We found a bird's nest!" Clara interrupted.

"And this cricket!" Katie-Belle thrust a specimen jar onto the Head Ranger's lap. "See how jumpy it is?"

"And you've just got to see our photo of a racoon." Clara dangled the camera in front of the Head Ranger again. "Mom says it was looking for

food, but another wild animal had already stolen our hot dogs!" She scowled at Evie.

"This is all very good," the Head Ranger said. "And I can see lots of detail in the photo of the racoon."

"That's because our camera has a telephoto lens!" Katie-Belle said, puffing out her chest.

The Head Ranger nodded. "I think it's the biggest mammal I've seen so far today. Well done, girls."

Iris glanced at Zak and Evie. "Er—I think we might have a mammal that is a little larger . . ."

CHAPTER 27

"Ha! I knew that moose picture would clinch it!" Zak said as they carried their winner's prize of camping goodies out of the cabin.

"Cheater!" cried a voice from behind them.

They turned to find the twins glaring at them.

"You must have cheated," Clara said, pointing a finger at Zak. "There's no way you could have taken that picture."

"He didn't cheat!" Iris snapped. "Zak really did

take that picture. But we know YOU tried to cheat. You took Evie's backpack! And I'm sure you deliberately wiped Zak's camera. And you probably untied Fudge's leash, too."

"Did not!" the twins said at the same time, their faces turning beet red.

"Whatever." Iris's eyes narrowed. "But you still lost. So now we just need to think of a suitable forfeit . . ." Iris looked at Evie and Zak. "Any ideas, guys?"

The twins looked a little nervous now.

"Well, I guess they could help out at the bookstore," Zak said. "There's always loads of shelf stacking to be done."

"Nah, too easy," Iris said.

The twins' faces turned redder.

"They could clean out Gammy's chicken sheds," Zak suggested. "They're always so poopy."

"Noooo!" the twins said together.

"We've got animal allergies," Clara added with a smug expression.

Evie was about to suggest they wash dishes at the Browns' diner. *But I'm not too sure Hannah would like to have you hanging around our kitchen. And I wouldn't, either!*

"I've got another idea . . . ," Iris said, winking at her friends. "Litter-picking on the beach tomorrow!"

"Ugh!" Katie-Belle cried. "Picking up someone else's trash? I'm NOT doing that."

"Oh, don't worry," Zak said. "Gammy will give you overalls and gloves so you'll be able to pick up all the really stinky, sticky, gooey stuff."

The twins grimaced.

"And trash bags," Iris added. "Gammy's got loads of them. So you can be busy all day! Gammy will be so pleased to have two more volunteers for the Lime Bay Litter Bugs. I'll tell her to expect you tomorrow, as soon as you get back from camping."

The twins glared at her for a moment, then stomped off.

"That was so funny," Zak said as they walked

back to their campsite. "Do you think they'll really show up?"

"Dunno!" Iris laughed. "It was worth it just to see their faces."

Evie giggled, too. But then her smile started to slide. She'd noticed the sun was going down; it was getting late, and she still didn't know whether Hannah was planning to leave. *If we do, we'll be back in Lime Bay long before the twins.*

"Look!" Iris said as they got closer to their campsite. "The lights are so pretty!"

The fairy lights the agents had strung around the tents were twinkling in the dusk, and the wind chimes had begun to tinkle in a slight breeze that ruffled Evie's hair.

"It looks so magical." Evie sighed. "I really hope we can stay."

"Check that out," Iris whispered, pointing to where Hannah was sitting with one of Beauty's colorful blankets around her shoulders and Fudge asleep by her feet. "They look awfully peaceful."

"And they've still not pumped the tires," Zak noted as they passed the vehicle.

Evie tried not to get too excited. Hannah *did* look relaxed. And her parents hadn't even begun to pack up the campsite . . . *Could Hannah have changed her mind?*

Fudge lifted his head at the sound of their footsteps, and he jumped up, his tail wagging as he let out a friendly *Hello-Evie-I'm-so-pleased-to-see-you* sort of a bark!

Hannah looked up, too, and smiled. "Oh wow!" she said as she spotted the box of camping goodies that Iris was holding. "I'm guessing you guys won the scavenger hunt."

"Congratulations!" Evie's dad walked over, a wide grin on his face. "Let's see your prize . . . Oh, very nice," he added, peering into the box. "Snacks, flashlights, a sleeping bag, luxury hot chocolate and—whoa, I love that kettle!"

Evie nodded, but she was still looking at her stepmom, trying to read her face. *Are we staying? Have you decided not to take Fudge to the shelter? Because you guys look kind of cozy together.*

"You should be so proud of yourselves," Hannah said, getting up and walking over to join them. "I know I am!" She reached out her hand and brushed the hair away from Evie's face. "I've been thinking . . ."

The bubble of hope inside Evie's tummy felt so large now, she thought she might float away.

". . . Maybe we shouldn't go home tonight," Hannah said. "I mean, Fudge has been so well-behaved while you've been gone. And you guys have made the campsite look so beautiful. And we've been listening to the most wonderful music . . . I'm not sure where it's coming from—I guess one of the other campsites . . ."

Evie glanced across the campfire and spotted Agent C and Agent S on the other side. Beauty had a little guitar on her lap. They both smiled at Evie and gave her a thumbs-up. Evie was relieved to see the other nine Agent Cs had disappeared now.

"So how about we stay here for the night," Hannah said. "And enjoy the slumber party, just like you guys suggested. We can eat some food—I loved the s'mores you made, by the way. And we can sing some songs, and tell stories and maybe do some star gazing and—" Hannah paused as a large blob of water hit her face. "Huh?" She looked up and another hit her eye. Followed by another, and then another . . .

"The storm!" Iris muttered. "Just like Agent R predicted."

In seconds the sky had turned black. The small blobs of rain became larger splotches, then suddenly it was sheeting down, bouncing off the tents and chairs as huge puddles began to form on the ground around the campfire.

"Everyone into the tents," Evie's dad called as he and Hannah rushed around, covering up the food and lifting the blankets from the chairs.

Evie grabbed Fudge and dived for their tent

while Zak and Iris wrestled the box of camping goodies in through the flap behind them.

"Room for two small ones?" Agent C said, poking her head through the flap moments later, and she and Agent S squished in next to the friends. "Ugh," Agent C groaned, "rain makes my hair so floppy."

Evie frowned. Something was nagging in the back of her mind . . . She looked at the agents and suddenly realized what it was. "Um—it's lovely to see you guys, but—er—how come you're still here? I mean, Hannah has just said we can stay, which means my wish has come true. And last time that happened, you disappeared back into the book."

"Mm, yes, that is strange." Agent C looked at Agent S. "Do you know why we're still here?"

"I'm not sure." Agent S rubbed her chin and scratched her ear. "Perhaps it's because—"

But she didn't get a chance to finish her sentence, because right at that moment Iris let out a squeal as a large gush of water fell on her head.

"It's raining INSIDE the tent!" she wailed, shaking the wet off her hair.

Zak reached up and touched the roof, and immediately another giant splatter of water poured through the canvas, landing on him.

"Guys!" Hannah shouted from the other tent. "I think the canvases must have moth holes. I'm so sorry, but I think we're going to have to go home after all."

What? Nooo! Evie couldn't believe what she was hearing. After everything they'd been through, they couldn't go home now. *Maybe we could shelter somewhere,* she thought, *just until the rain has passed. And then maybe Agent S could mend the tents with her sewing machine or perhaps she could make new tents . . .* She was about to ask the agents for help, when Fudge's ears pricked up. He cocked his head, listening to something, then gave a little bark, dived across Evie's lap, and headed straight out through the tent flap.

"Stop!" Evie cried, trying to grab his leash. But Fudge was too fast.

She scrambled outside after him. But he'd taken off, racing across the campsite and out into the darkness, until he disappeared into the trees.

CHAPTER 28

"Come back!" Evie hollered. "FUDGE!"

For a second, Evie just stood there, blinking as the rain made her eyes all blurry. *I should tell Hannah and Dad what's happened. But if I do, Hannah will change her mind about staying and then everything will be ruined. I've got to get him back before they notice!* She poked her head back into her tent. "Pass me one of those flashlights," she said. "I'm going after him."

"I'll come, too," Zak said.

"And me!" Iris grabbed another flashlight and crawled out after her cousin. "So which way did he go?"

"This way!" Evie shouted over the noise of the rain, and they set off toward the trees, their feet squelching on the soaking grass and slipping in the mud.

"Wait for us!" Agent C shouted as she and Agent S followed behind.

"Evie?" Hannah was out of her tent now, too. "Where are you going?"

But Evie didn't hear. She had only one thing on her mind. *I've got to get Fudge back!*

"Which way now?" Iris yelled, wiping the rain out of her eyes.

They'd reached the thicker woods, and the path had vanished.

"I don't know." Evie glanced around, pushing her wet hair out of her face. She shivered. Her drenched clothes were sticking to her, making every step much heavier.

Zak crouched down and shone his flashlight along the track. "Paw prints! Look, over there!—I'm sure they're Fudge's. Come on . . . this way."

They followed the prints through the dark trees with Zak's flashlight. All around were strange noises, rustlings, scrabbling, the sound of twigs breaking. And then another sound—

"That's Fudge!" Evie shouted. "I'd know his bark anywhere!—FUDGE?" she yelled. "Where are you, boy?"

"That way!" Iris pointed off to the left, and they pushed their way through the trees and bushes as the woofing got louder and closer . . . And then—

"There he is!" Evie shouted.

They'd reached a clearing now, and they spotted the pup diving around at the bottom of a giant tree.

"About time, too!" shouted a voice from high up in the branches. And suddenly Agent R somersaulted down onto the ground in front of them.

"What on earth—" Evie began.

Rapunzel bent down and tickled Fudge's ears. "Awesome work, Agent Dog!" She looked at Evie. "As soon as I started whistling for him, he appeared. Just like last time."

"But why did you want Fudge?" Evie asked, wiping the rain out of her eyes.

"Because I knew you'd follow him. And I wanted to show you this!" She pointed up into the branches of the tree.

"I don't see—" Evie began.

But then Zak shone his flashlight upward, and suddenly she did.

"A treehouse?" Evie breathed.

"More like a tree palace!" Iris said, her eyes wide as she peered up at the two-story wooden building, with its heart-shaped windows and spiral staircase that wound down around the trunk.

Agent R puffed out her chest. "I told you, I was building something big and tall."

AGENT R'S TOP TREEHOUSE GUIDE

Listen up! Building treehouses is strictly for super-strong Agents of H.E.A.R.T. like me. (And a few regular grown-ups with tools and know-how.) But here's a mini treehouse for toys that anyone can make. (Even Agent C without her wand!)

You will need:

- A short, stocky fallen tree branch (the knobbier the better)

- String

- Twigs

- Old brown cardboard

- Brown paper

- A small cardboard box

- Glue

- Sticky tape

- A pencil and paint

- Safety scissors

- A large plant pot filled with soil, sand, or pebbles

- Pine cones, flowers, leaves, bark, or petals to decorate

How to make:

- Put your tree branch in the plant pot. Fill with soil, sand, or pebbles to hold the branch in place.

- Break off any thin shoots at the top of the branch to create a flattish area where your treehouse will eventually sit.

- Use old cardboard to make a platform to go at the top of your branch. This will be for your treehouse to sit on.

- Lay the platform over the top of the branch, and if there are branch stumps poking up, you will be able to use them to attach the platform by poking

holes through the cardboard and pushing the platform down onto them.

- You can create holes by first lining up the platform and marking where the stumps are with a pencil, then placing the cardboard on the ground and poking the holes through with your safety scissors.

- Now secure your platform onto the top of your branch.

- Make a little house to fit on top of the platform. You can make one from LEGO blocks or use a small carboard box, which you could paint or decorate with paper.

- If you want to make a roof for your small box, you can cut off the flaps from one end (if it has flaps), and tape them together to make a V shape, then glue or stick to your box to form a roof.

- You could also use cardboard to make a

roof. Fold a piece into a V shape and attach to the box.

- Paint or color your treehouse.

- Place the house on top of the platform. Cover with moss, leaves, or petals.

- Make a rope ladder and swing by tying small twigs together with string.

- For the rope ladder, break twigs into five small, equal pieces, approx. 2-3 inches (6-8 centimeters), then cut two 12-inch (30-centimeter, approx.) pieces of string. Start with one piece of string and tie it to the twigs at one end, with equal gaps between the twigs to create the steps of the ladder. Then use the other piece of string to repeat at the other end of the twigs. Hook the ladder onto your tree branch or tie it on.

- For the swing, tie two pieces of string to

either end of a short, thick twig and attach to the branch.

- Decorate the treehouse and the soil/pebbles/sand in your plant pot with twigs, pine cones, leaves, petals, bark, or anything else you can find in the yard.

- Add your favorite toys or mini figures.

- If you want to make it even more snazzy, plant a garden for your toys in the soil around the treehouse. Dig up a few weeds or little flowers and replant them in the soil. Or you could plant a few seeds around the tree branch . . . mini sunflowers or daisies would look awesome. You can also make your toys a pond by digging a hole in the soil, placing a small plant pot into it, and filling the pot with water.

"And it's not a prison for my parents?" Evie asked.

Agent R snorted. "No! It's a shelter. See, I knew the storm was coming, and you'd need a proper place to spend the night. Though if you want to lock your parents inside, you could just take away the staircase, unless either of them has got long hair, because—"

"If you don't have a stair," Agent C said, arriving at that moment . . .

". . . just use your hair!" Agent S finished off as she appeared next to her.

The three agents high-fived one another.

"I LOVE it!" Agent S said, peering up at the treehouse, and a little red embroidered heart appeared above her head and lit up the sky.

"EVIE? Where are you?"

"That's Hannah!" Evie whispered. "Do you think she'll agree to stay here?"

Agent R grinned. "Of course she will! Who wouldn't swap a leaky tent for a cozy treehouse?" She winked at Evie, then vanished.

And when Evie turned around, she realized the other two agents had gone, too.

"Evie?" her stepmom was first into the clearing, closely followed by her dad.

"We were so worried . . ." Hannah put her arms around Evie and hugged her. "It's far too dark now to go off by yourself. You must be so cold."

Evie took a deep breath and crossed her fingers. "Um—I've got something special to show you guys . . ."

EPILOGUE

Sometime later, after everyone had moved their backpacks into the treehouse for the night and munched their way through the slumber party food, it was time for flashlights out.

Hannah had one last look around, then climbed into her sleeping bag. "Do you think this is a facility organized by the Head Ranger?" she asked Evie's dad. "It's so fancy!"

"Sure," he replied, snuggling into his blankets. "A lot of campgrounds offer treehouses now. I'll go settle up with Ranger Alex tomorrow."

Evie coughed. "I guess we're really lucky Fudge found this place, right?" she called down from the mezzanine level above, where the three friends and Fudge were bedding down for the night.

Hannah chuckled. "Yes, this time Fudge's exuberance definitely saved the day!"

"So . . . um—I was wondering . . ." Evie looked at her friends and crossed her fingers. "Does this mean Fudge can stay?"

There was a moment of silence in the treehouse. Evie held her breath, picturing her parents exchanging glances. *Please, Hannah. Please say he can.*

"I don't know, honey . . . ," Hannah began.

"How about a trial run," Evie's dad called up. "Maybe we should give Fudge a week. And if he settles in and doesn't cause too much chaos, perhaps we could think about making it permanent."

Evie could barely breathe waiting for her step-mom to reply.

"Okay, I agree," Hannah said. "Let's review things in a week."

Evie thought her face would crack with the size of her smile. Iris and Zak were grinning, too. They gave her a thumbs-up, and Iris mouthed, "You did it!"

"Thanks, Hannah. Thanks, Dad," Evie mumbled, on account of suddenly feeling a little tearful. "Fudge won't let you down. I promise."

The pup gave a tiny yelp, as though he really wouldn't, and Evie snuggled him closer.

As she lay back, the sound of the rain outside, combined with the fresh, comforting scent of the wood in their shelter, began to make her eyelids droop. "I was thinking," Evie said. "Maybe when we get back to the diner, we could make a treehouse-themed dessert, with chocolate fingers and toffee sauce and little hearts made out of raspberries . . ."

She heard her parents chuckle.

"Nice idea," Hannah called from below. "But now it's time for sleep . . . Goodnight, guys."

"'Night!" they all chorused back.

Zak reached over to turn off their flashlight. "So we're all agreed," he whispered. "No one will ever mention me wearing this again, right?"

They'd found the sparkly onesies that Sleeping Beauty had made for them, folded up inside Evie's backpack. And strangely, they were the only dry clothes in the whole tent.

"Sure," Evie said. "Pinkie promise!"

Iris grinned. "I don't know . . . it depends how super annoying you are in the future!"

"Pax!" Evie whispered, before the argument could get going. Then she rolled onto her side and felt to make sure the magical book was still under her pillow where she'd put it as soon as they'd moved into the treehouse. After losing it earlier, she was never going to let it out of her sight again. Then she closed her eyes and drifted off to sleep. And the magical book glistened softly in the darkness.

ACKNOWLEDGMENTS

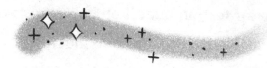

Teamwork is essential when camping, and so, too, when making a book.

I'd like to thank the sparkling team at Feiwel and Friends who use their magical powers to bring Evie and her adventures alive. And especially my wonderful editor, Holly West, for her fantastic suggestions, endless wisdom, and brilliant advice.

Thanks also to Genevieve Kote, our talented artist, for her enchanting illustrations.

As ever, I'm grateful to my publishing fairy god-mother, agent Gemma Cooper, for her boundless energy, enthusiasm, and support.

But most of all I'd like to thank my family, without whom I'd never write a word. Thanks to Archie for the camping and nature advice you gave me. And to Alice for testing out all of Evie's bakes and makes, and for loving this series so much.

And finally, thanks to my readers, for sharing Evie's story. Sending twinkly, magical wishes to you all.